WEAVING IN THE ENDS

K. M. HERKES

Print edition:
ISBN-10:1-945745-00-2
ISBN-13:978-1-945745-00-3
Electronic edition:
ISBN-10: 1-945745-010
ISBN-13: 978-1945745-010

Cover Design Rhonda Zatezalo
based on original by Rachel Bostwick

Dawnrigger Publishing, Illinois USA
August 2016

BOOKS BY K. M. HERKES

Stories of the Restoration

In recommended reading order

Controlled Descent

Flight Plan

Weaving In the Ends

Novices

Rollover

Rough Passages

The Sharp Edge of Yesterday

WEAVING IN THE ENDS

DEDICATIONS

Paul, without you I would be only a dreamer, not a writer. Your steadfast support made this happen. No dedication, no acknowledgement, no words will ever be sufficient to express my gratitude and love.

Berni, Blynn, Cathy, Dan, Deb, Doug, Emily, Hugh, John, Lisa, Lynn, Susan, Tess—you are all awesome, and I want the world to know it. At various points in the gestation of this novel, each of you offered critical feedback, monumental editing help, necessary encouragement, or pivotal plotting solutions.
Thank you all.

TURNING THE WORK

EVERY STORY STARTS SOMEWHERE

At the beginning of *Turning the Work*, we find private investigator Carl Jenson and his brother Eddie Parker doing what they do best: working too hard.

They're supposed to be taking it easy.

Almost a year ago, they helped a brilliant but eccentric inventor track down shadowy enemies who wanted him dead at any cost. They solved the mystery and saved the day, but victory came with a high personal price. Recuperation from catastrophic injuries has kept them both busy for months.

Now they have a new undercover case conveniently tied into Parker's continuing occupational therapy, and life is looking up. The problem: administrative complications have put the investigation on hold, and neither brother knows what to do with leisure time.

Parker's physical therapist is the only person more frustrated by the situation than they are. Being a clever woman who knows when she's beaten, she gives her patient some homework...

CHAPTER 1
MONDAY JULY 6

CARL WAS PUTTING AWAY laundry when the door to his apartment opened and then slammed shut. By the time he got out of the bedroom, his brother was already on the living room couch, bent forward with his head resting on his knees.

Parker sat like that for several moments, tall body curled over folded arms, breathing slowly and evenly. Then he eased gingerly back until his shoulders sank deep into the cushions. His hair was the same shade as the rich brown fabric. His face was pale brown with sickly gray undertones.

"Fucking hell," he whispered. Then he put his boots up onto the coffee table. Monday post-therapy ritual: complete.

Carl brought over a bottle of beer from the kitchen. "So? What's the news from hell today?"

Parker cracked open one bloodshot hazel eye and then the other, then shut both eyes again and growled. That meant *too tired to shove that bottle down your throat and make you chew on it. Lucky you.*

Carl set the beer on the table and took a seat on the nearby weight bench. His ability to interpret body language as easily as speech didn't make awkward conversations any easier. Anger was problematic. Parker usually worked it off using his fists, but the fists were the source of his aggravation now. Carl hazarded a guess about the cause. "Did Naomi drop the fit-enough-for-normal-activities speech on you? That's too bad. Things were going so well."

A small, betraying squirm indicated that Carl was looking in the right direction but from the wrong angle. He corrected himself: "She chewed you out for overtraining. Good for her. I warned you, didn't I?"

Judging from Parker's grimace, his physical therapist had raked him over the coals and flayed him bloody for pushing his healing body too hard, too fast. Carl's lack of sympathy earned him a bleak glare that he translated as, *She's allowed to nag. You aren't. My arms might be useless, but I can still kick your ass.*

"Oh, try it, please." Frustration bled into Carl's voice. A year and a half spent supporting a competitive high-energy convalescent would be enough to try the patience of a saint. He was no saint, and his psychiatric training couldn't prevent emotional burnout any more than Parker's unarmed combat skills could have prevented him from being nearly crippled in a fight where he was overmatched and outnumbered. Skill only went so far.

Professional expertise only meant Carl understood why his patience was wearing thin. It didn't stop the chafing. He stood and stepped up close. "You want a fight? Go ahead, take a swing. I dare you, brother mine."

Parker wasn't short by any measure, but Carl was taller. These days he had more than the usual advantage of fifteen kilos of muscle and a longer reach. He also had two working hands. Parker couldn't even hold a beer bottle. It wouldn't be a fair contest, and Carl didn't care in the least.

The bitterness in Parker's eyes slowly lightened to dry humor. A deliberate examination started at Carl's feet and ended two meters up with a smirk mocking Carl's shoulder-length blond hair. *No thanks, pretty boy,* was the silent jeer. *You need a fuck, not a fight.*

Carl grabbed the last shreds of his temper before they tore completely and exposed the guilt and frustrated helplessness lurking beneath. "I need you to start working more than your arm muscles. One day you're going to wake up and find out your vocal cords have totally atrophied. I can read silences. The rest of the world can't."

As if I care, was Parker's sniffed response, followed by a huff of breath that acknowledged the point. "Can't get range of motion on the damned off-hand," he said after a long silence. "She wants me to try knitting."

"Knitting?" Carl thought he must've heard it wrong. "Why?"

Parker lifted one shoulder. *Does it matter?*

The full subtext there was *Anything Naomi suggests is worth a try,* and that trust was reason enough for Carl to support the only therapist willing to deal with Parker's temper for more than two sessions. "All right, knitting it is. Did she give you any directions? An idea where to start?"

A shrug, both shoulders.

"You're killing me here. Words. Please."

"She gave me lists and shit. Exercises. Equipment to buy." The response was prompt, quiet, and carried a full measure of apology along with a dose of resentment. The result looked like *I am trying* balanced with *Cut me some slack. I nursed you for five years, asshole.*

Carl answered, "You nursed me for a few weeks. Worrying

about my sanity all those years doesn't count. Besides, I got over it. You'll get through this. Shut up and drink your damned beer."

Parker reached for the bottle, slowly lifting it with his left hand and keeping the right one ready in case he lost his grip. The maneuver was more than a little wobbly. His ability to pick up anything at all was still a marvel, considering that several surgeries had been required to replace shattered bones from elbows to fingertips.

An incoming message alert distracted Carl from the everyday miracle. He checked the screen on his wristband and said, "Naomi's taking me up on my offer to help wrangle you. She must be worried."

The note read, "If your brother keeps straining the elbow rebuild with push-ups I will not waste my time or his. Please stop him. Also, if he ever wants to roll a knife again without losing fingers he needs more fine-motor practice. His eyes glaze over when I give him instructions. I'm forwarding you some files."

Carl looked up to find Parker watching him with sharp interest, and the obvious hit him right between the eyes. *Someone's desperate to get laid,* he thought to himself. *But it isn't me.*

All he said aloud was, "We'll go shopping tomorrow."

DAWN FOUND THEM BOTH in Golden Gate Park with a group of t'ai chi practitioners, moving quietly in cool damp until the gray shadows brightened to emerald green and the mist lifted on a glowing blue morning. Afterwards Carl hiked back to the apartment to kill time while Parker entertained himself training other people's dogs for a couple of hours.

Breakfast didn't take long, so Carl did a little preliminary research while he waited. It wasn't a thrilling way to pass the time, but there were good things to be said about mundane and ordinary. Boredom had a certain appeal after the excitement they'd seen in recent years.

Once Parker got back, it was time to head through the city to the closest knitting supply shop. A good hike took them into the Mission district, past an eclectic mix of restored historic buildings and newer ones built over the damage left after a double-decade of urban turmoil.

San Francisco's restoration efforts in the fifty years since the worst battles and riots had brought the city back to life. The scars still showed, but the result was a vibrant, healthy community. It was a walking town, and the sidewalks were well-populated both with summer vacationers and locals whose jobs allowed them free hours in the daylight.

Carl liked the atmosphere. People were friendly, not with cloying small-town intrusiveness but with an active, all-embracing tolerance. Parker spent a lot of time turning to walk backwards so he could take a second guess on sexual identity, but most of the smiles Carl saw were genuine, and he thought he could get used to the sense of universal acceptance.

Knotty Issues was squeezed between a café and a local council office on the ground floor of a corner building. Four stories of apartments rose above the commercial tenants, and there was apparently a competition in progress for biggest flower box and largest decorative flag.

The shop door was propped open, and swirls of chalk on the sidewalk echoed patterns painted over the picture window around the store name. The artwork blocked any view of the interior from the street and vice versa. That security faux pas left Parker eying the place with suspicion. Carl grabbed him by the back of his shirt when he started to walk away.

"Oh, no you don't. If you chicken out, I will rat on you to Naomi."

The threat stopped Parker in his tracks. He shrugged to settle his shirt collar, raised his chin, and stomped into the place. *Asshole.*

Inside, Carl's first impression was one of dazzling color and crowded confusion. He hunched before he could stop himself, shoulders rounding and spine slumping forward. He channeled the tension down and out, exhaling it before it could build into panic. A second deep breath quelled the claustrophobia. It wasn't a small space. It was only a full one.

The overhead lights were bright and the walls white, but the cramped feel of too many things packed into too little space overwhelmed their cheery efforts. A counter ran across the window frontage, full divided shelves filled both side walls up to a four-meter high ceiling, and a long wooden table in the center of the floor left only narrow aisles for moving past merchandise. At the rear, an archway strung with hanging decorations led into another room.

Six women sat at the table with hands moving busily over and under bits of thin yarn. Knitting, Carl assumed, although he didn't see needles. After cursory glances at the new arrivals they continued a quiet but spirited discussion about sourdough bread without missing a beat.

Parker had ground to a halt in front of a large metal washtub full of fluffy puffs dyed in neon hues. He glanced sidelong as Carl caught up. *Now what?*

Carl shrugged, and Parker headed for the rear of the shop to scout for exits and hidden threats. Carl gave the crew at the table a second look and was ignored a second time, so he took his time making a closer examination of the shop.

Yarn in every conceivable texture, color and thickness was everywhere, spilling off the edges of the higher shelves, lying in piles on the table and nestled in baskets on the counter. It was even strung and looped over the tops of the seats. Carl curled his fingers into his palms as a reminder to keep his hands to himself. The rainbow parade of textures invited tactile exploration, but he already felt large and clumsy and out of place. Better safe than sorry.

Some of the implements in bins on the lower shelves and in decorative containers on benches were recognizable from his perfunctory studies. The rest, like most of the assorted larger devices and freestanding equipment visible through the archway, were wholly outside his experience.

"What the fuck is this?" Parker said from somewhere in back, and the voices at the table fell silent. Five of the six women looked up at Carl, and he felt a tickle of amusement at the nearly identical expressions on their faces.

The messages were variations on a theme. *Rude. Ignorant. Unwelcome. Inappropriate. Offensive.* Underlying all the disapproval was a single irrefutable accusation: *Male.*

Carl's amusement grew from a tickle to mischievous impulse. He pasted on the best oblivious smile in his repertoire and sauntered past all the rejection with more than a little swagger in his step. "How the fuck would I know what it is, asshole?" he called back to Parker. "What the fuck are you looking at?"

The unrepentant spray of expletives won him five audible huffs and five offended glares. The condemnation on four lined faces under gray thinning hair was nothing more than the blanket dismissal of callow immaturity by aging authority. The fifth face was barely adult, brunette and pretty, and her bristling was more about status than indignation. *I belong. You don't.*

The sixth woman continued smiling down at the material in her hands as she'd been doing the entire time. She was closer in age to the youngster than the elders, but laugh lines around her eyes and mouth cheerfully admitted maturity.

She was intriguing. The inattentiveness was an act, disguising a possessive awareness of her surroundings that pegged her as the proprietor or at least an employee. Ignoring new customers while the current ones attempted to chase them off seemed like a recipe for commercial failure, but the choice was deliberate. Carl could tell that much at a glance.

He gave her a nod in passing. Her body was far from petite and closer to sturdy than lush, and short black hair hinted at impatience with appearances while a tailored jacket acknowledged their importance. The overall declaration was a blend of *I know what I like* and *What you see is what you get.*

The brash attitude more than made up for a face too strong to be considered pretty, but it didn't explain her aloofness. And none of it was any of Carl's business, so he kept on moving. He was here to keep Parker on task, not to entertain himself with attractive mysteries.

The quiet noise of hands in motion announced *vulgarity will now be ignored* behind him. The conversation muttered back to life as he ducked under low-hanging obstacles in the archway.

The back room was twice as wide as the front. Shelves full of books framed seating areas with thick rugs and standing work lights. The chairs all looked a little fragile, but a worn leather couch had been pushed against the side wall under another painted-over window. Carl sank into it and stretched out both legs.

The fleece rug glowed with color-stained sunlight from the high windows, and it squished thickly underfoot as if inviting him to take off his boots. He smiled, considering the reaction from the biddies up front, and he put his feet up on the table instead.

Parker was examining an elaborate cage-like contraption that took up most of one corner. It was a dangerous-looking piece of work packed with sharp metal protrusions and lots of overlapping moving parts. The lethal appearance was more than impressive enough to explain his startled comment earlier.

"That's a loom," Carl told him and received an incredulous over-the-shoulder stare. *How the hell do you know that?*

"Naomi gave you lists, remember? You could've done your own intelligence-gathering, you know. Or you could try reading." Carl pointed at the signs on the wall: pricing and rental options for spinning wheels, carding machines, looms and more. "Look, they even have pictures."

Parker shot him a dirty look, but a wood-handled tool with multiple sharp tines soon distracted him. He tested the points with his hand and hissed. One finger went into his mouth, and his eyes tracked back to Carl. *What. The. Fuck?*

Carl sighed. "Wool comb."

And? said the curious eyebrows. Carl reminded himself to stop enabling the silence and gritted his teeth. Finally Parker said aloud, "What's it for?"

"No idea. I would assume it combs wool, whatever that means. They come in pairs."

Parker's sniff expressed his dissatisfaction. He continued his haphazard explorations, braving the front section now and again, touching everything as he went. Carl picked up a printed book of patterns and leafed through it.

The instructions reminded him of a mathematics text: the words looked normal, but none of them connected in expected ways. He hoped that the instructions would make more sense once the code was mastered, the way equations did. Otherwise they were totally screwed.

Parker brought over a selection of tools and spilled them onto the table, then crouched down and arranged them for review. *What do you think?*

Carl regarded the collection as objectively as possible. He considered and rejected several lines of inquiry before settling on, "Are you planning to knit something or assassinate someone?"

A warm voice nearby said, "I was wondering that myself."

Carl tensed, and the edges of the book in his hands crumpled slightly. Parker shot to his feet, but he recovered fast and settled his face in a polite mask. The strain across his shoulders was the only thing that betrayed the internal shift from standby to red alert. Almost the only thing. Carl reached over and removed the knitting needle from his brother's grasp. Just in case.

The proprietor crossed her arms and leaned casually against the curve of the archway. "Can I help you make up your mind? It is my shop, after all."

Her eyes were a warm, light brown that was a close match to her skin tone. Her smile revealed crooked teeth and a wry sense of humor. "Sorry about the hankie hags. They're gone now, so I can give you boys a hand if you want."

Parker could do an excellent imitation of a helpless puppy when he put the work into it. He sat down beside Carl and gave it his best shot. "Please?"

"Sure thing." The proprietor walked over to assess Parker's choices and bent over the table with a twinkle in her eye that said, *You want to play? Let's play.*

Parker knew how to flirt with every well-toned muscle in his body. He was tall and chiseled from top to toe, but that was least of it. Frank sexuality and candid admiration could make words all but superfluous.

The woman's reaction demonstrated appreciation for the game rather than serious interest. Practical, independent, professionally successful but personally vulnerable to rejection; she was used to picking her own partners to avoid being refused, and Parker wasn't her type.

And none of those points were ones she was consciously sharing. Carl caught himself short again. Parker wasn't the only one who'd gotten lazy over the last year. It took concentration to keep from looking for the cues and tells that revealed more than people intended to disclose, and distraction was affecting his self-control.

His mind might work better if a pair of stupendous breasts weren't on display less than a meter in front of his nose. The jacket wasn't tight enough to keep things from swaying when the woman moved, and she wasn't wearing a bra.

He needed to keep his analytic tendencies on a tight leash and his mouth shut or he was going to end up talking his way into a total stranger's bed before he even had a chance to do a background check. Parker would never let him live that down, which was reason enough to avoid the complication. He couldn't think of any other reasons at the moment.

The woman shook her head and picked up everything except the mate to the needle Carl was still holding. "Which is it, girlfriend or gory accident?"

Parker looked to Carl for a translation, but he could only shrug in equal confusion. "Excuse me?"

Her gaze darted between the two of them, reassessing. *Disappointed.* "Oh, is it boyfriend? Are you looking for gifts for a friend, or finishing up some kind of physical therapy for a hand or wrist injury? Those are the usual two reasons clueless newbies end up here."

She meant male ones by that, and resignation pressed sharply through the pleasant alto voice like a knife wrapped in silk. She loved her job, but it had its drawbacks.

Carl deflected Parker's elbow before it hit his ribs, caught the man's wrist, and used grip strength that sent its own kind of silent message. *My social life is none of your business.*

Parker sat there and radiated *but you seriously need to get laid,* and Carl briefly considered fratricide. He settled for redirection. "What are hankie hags?"

"It's a club. They're tatters. They tat? Tatting? Lace-making?" The woman looked relieved when she finally found a description that crossed the jargon barrier. "I'm trying to learn, and they're brilliant. They are also insufferable, but Tuesday mornings are so slow that I don't even schedule staff until eleven. And that's enough about me. What brings you here?"

That was a question Carl had no intention of answering. He pointed at Parker, who raised both hands and wiggled his fingers. "Gory accident. No boyfriends. No girlfriends."

His smile edged past the bounds of good manners and jumped happily into lecherous appreciation.

The woman grinned back. "Well, then. Good to know. Either knitting or crochet will build up strength and coordination. I'll get you started with the basics. Who knows, you might end up enjoying it. A girl can hope, right?"

At the end her eyes moved to Carl, and the smile she gave him carried a cheerful, unaffected invitation to join in the game.

Carl smiled back before he thought twice about it. She reacted with a delighted grin as honest and direct as every other emotion the woman projected. She held out a hand to Parker for a brief, silent—careful—handclasp, then extended it to Carl. "Felicity Chen. Nice to meet you both."

Her grip was firm, and she held on long enough to make her point clear when her fingers lingered on their retreat. *Hello, handsome,* said the light touch against Carl's wrist, generating a response as immediate as an electric shock.

The sensation didn't make any side trips on its travels south. Nerve to nerve to nerve, no interference from the brain at all. Carl knew the sinking feeling he was feeling was his sanity drowning in hormones. He decided he didn't care.

He met those sweet brown eyes and smiled again. "I'm Carl Harris. The would-be knitter here is my brother Parker."

"All right, then. Good to meet you both. I'll be happy to get you started with—" A bell rang in the front of the store, and Felicity turned. "Sorry, I have to get that."

She spoke over her shoulder as she headed for the door. "I'll be right back. Give me a second? Better yet, come up front to the worktable. It's safe now."

The sway of hips as she walked off was both deliberate and practiced, a particular bit of body language as old as time and as subtle as a brick through a window. She still had zero expectations of going further than flirtation, but hope was something else again.

Parker went after her, pausing for a last look back at Carl from the archway. *Why are you still sitting there? Move, moron.*

He moved.

FELICITY WAS BUSY CORRECTING a careless counting error when the front door chimed. She heard Abby's greeting to the courier, and she smiled at the cheerful sound of Miriam's bracelets jingling. The subsequent bustle of boxed orders being sent out for delivery followed right on schedule.

Good employees were a blessing to be cherished. Felicity settled deeper into the couch and returned to the task of unraveling rows. Music wafted through the room, the breeze from the open window was warm, she had a belly full of excellent curry, and a cherry slushie was slowly melting on the coffee table.

Life was good. If she could pick out her mistake without snagging the yarn, life would be nearly perfect.

"Hey, Flee! Come out here, will you? Someone has a question for you."

Miriam didn't sound worried, but she wouldn't interrupt if it wasn't important. The house rule was that lunch hours were sacrosanct. Picturing a customer-service crisis or an ordering dilemma, Felicity picked up her workbag and hurried to the front.

The bag slipped from her grip when she got to the archway and surprise left her momentarily numb.

It wasn't an emergency. Far from it. *This day just keeps getting better and better.* Carl Harris stood beside Felicity's worktable with his arms crossed over his broad chest and his khaki shirt looking a little strained around the seams.

Felicity hadn't gotten any further than staring at the contact information he'd left with her yet. Flirting was her comfort zone. Taking the next step was asking for hurt feelings, and she'd still been building up courage to call him. Now here he was, right in front of her like an uptight genie summoned by her hopeful daydreams.

His brother Parker was poking through a selection of knitting needles on the sales counter with Abby's assistance. She looked worried. Parker looked angry. Felicity looked at Carl. He was close enough to touch, not that she would, but it meant she had to look up.

Very few people made her feel dainty. Carl was one of them. He didn't stand next to things so much as loom over whatever was nearby. That was a delightful experience for any woman reconciled to towering over dance partners, and while the brother was easy on the eyes, all earth tones and energy, Carl was scrumptious like fresh apple pie. Adding eyes of sunset blue and shaggy blond hair that begged to be finger-combed to the package was like getting ice cream and caramel on top of the extra-large slice. *Yum.*

Carl picked up the overflowing workbag and handed it to her. "Is that what a doily should look like? Parker's first attempt looked like dog vomit."

His deep soft-spoken comment brushed away the daydreams, and Felicity's face warmed as she hurriedly tucked away the project. It wasn't a doily. She'd agreed to knit lingerie on a dare from Miriam. *Not explaining that, no.*

"I didn't expect to see you back," was what came out of her mouth, and she winced inside. "I mean, I'm surprised to see you back already."

"I could tell," Carl said. "Here's hoping it's a pleasant surprise. If Parker doesn't get some help, we're not going to survive the weekend. He's picking up a new set of needles now. Can you recommend a tutor?"

"Me. I love teaching." A legitimate excuse. Just what she needed. *Thank you universe, thank you, thank you, thank you.* Doubt crept in to tug at elation's skirts. "Why is he looking at new needles? If he doesn't like the ones he bought, I'll be happy to swap them out."

Carl hesitated before answering. Then his lips twitched, and his right shoulder went up and down in a little shrug. "I'm going to have to buy a pair of pliers to pry the steel ones out of the bedroom door, and I will let Parker explain what happened to the wood pair. Nothing left to trade in."

His eyes were sad above a wry smile as he added, "I don't suppose you still want the tutoring job?"

Felicity knew she should dive at the chance to retract her offer. She'd already seen enough red flags to line a Chinese New Year parade route, from the hair-trigger reactions both men displayed to the aura of lethal competence Parker wore the way some men splashed on cologne. According to the routine search she'd run, both men were construction subcontractors. She didn't believe that for a second. If they were electricians, then she was a fashion model.

Retreat was the sane response to being informed that her prospective client was a destructive maniac as well as a fraud.

She couldn't do it. The element of mystery was as tempting as a sprinkle of spice on that great big slice of pie a la mode.

She smiled back at Carl and said, "Of course I want it. I love a challenge."

They had secrets? Fine. She knew people who knew people who specialized in secrets.

Life is short, she told herself. *Eat dessert first.*

CHAPTER 4
MORNING, SATURDAY JULY 11

FOG WAS EVIL. CARL had been working up to that
conclusion for a few weeks now. Only malicious intent could
explain the way simple water vapor made life a total misery.
Damp cold was cruel to damaged joints and hard on skin stiffened by scarring. No matter how he dressed, the moisture crept
under every layer of clothing and left him soggy and sore all
over.

He should've known that the good weather of the past few
days wouldn't last, but Felicity evidently brought out the stupid
in him. She'd suggested meeting after Parker's daily workout in
the dog park, and Carl had agreed without a second thought.

Now he tucked his chin into his coat collar and tried to find
a comfortable position on the park bench. The service dogs and
their trainers were shadows inside a gray cloud. Whistles,
shouts, and a lot of barking from the trainees proved that the visibility was hampering instruction. He wouldn't even to be able to
see Felicity coming. If she came.

Carl shoved down doubts raised by aggravation and pain.
Felicity would've called if she wasn't going to show. Then again,

she might have only contacted Parker, and failure to pass along a message would be typical. Carl stood up to go see if he needed to kick his brother in the ass.

Felicity's arrival averted the necessity. A voice called out a greeting and a query to the group of trainers. One of the shadows identified itself as Parker with a casual wave and pointed uphill. Then Carl heard a humming voice and heels thumping confidently on the paved walk.

His mood lifted to absurd heights when a tall shadow appeared in the gloom. Giddiness was a serious danger sign. He was asking himself *what happened to the idea of an uncomplicated roll in the hay?* When Felicity got close enough to see details.

Moisture beaded her hair under a broad-brimmed hat that gave her a rakish air, and she wore a black coat that Carl coveted on sight. It covered her from chin to ankles, flaring out as she moved, shedding water with every step.

She stopped and stared, then held out a carrier with three travel cups. "Quick, take one before you freeze solid. I thought I was being silly to bring coffee, but you look like the world's biggest cat in a bathtub full of ice water."

Carl wrapped stiff fingers around the hot cup and shivered as he sat down again. "My savior. Thank you."

Felicity lifted a second cup and chuckled quietly as she took a sip. "So much for a nice morning in the fresh air. By the time I realized it was this bad I was almost here. I should've suggested a rendezvous at the café where I got these. They're used to crafters and students. Might be boring for you, though."

She sat down beside Carl with her thigh pressed close, but she remained stiff rather than settling into sync with him. *Anxious more than excited,* was Carl's interpretation.

She'd chosen public neutral ground for the meeting, a sign of intelligent caution, but the idea had misfired and she was expecting rejection. *Go ahead, make excuses and leave,* her body said.

Carl said, "Someone has to be a buffer between Parker's temper and the innocent bystanders." His posture and tone sent an additional message. *Relax, I'm not going anywhere.*

She relaxed, the relief exposing another brief glimpse of those hidden insecurities. "This kind of weather makes me miss Oregon," she said. "That's where I grew up. At least rain is honest. Fog is sneaky."

"I was just thinking the same thing." Carl mentally recited *keep it casual, keep it simple* even as he surrendered to idiocy and liberated the smile that wanted to spread across his face. "I feel like a wet cat."

Felicity said sympathetically, "Let's get you indoors and dry you out. How much longer will he be over there?"

Carl checked the time. "They'll be done any minute now."

"You really should get a coat that goes down past your thighs if you're going to stick around through August. How long are you in town?"

"I never said I was from out of town," he pointed out.

They'd gotten an alert when Felicity ran her check on their false identities. Parker's response had been: "Smart. Good." Which pretty much summed up Carl's feelings. It would still be nice to know how much she'd learned. One of her relatives was in Armed Forces Intelligence, so she had better than average resources.

Felicity took another sip and watched him over the top of her cup. "Oops."

"I would've been disappointed if you hadn't checked." Carl worked to keep the mood light. "I ran a records check too."

"It pays to be careful." Her tone carried a touch of asperity: she *had* tugged on the family connections, and at the very least she knew the public records were bogus. She didn't raise the issue, saying only, "I have three older brothers, by the way. All combat veterans and believe it or not, looking at me, worried about my safety."

The unspoken message was tossed out like a gauntlet. *I'm not naïve or stupid, and I have backup. Leave now if you can't handle competence and confidence.* It took a lot of rejection to build up emotional defenses that prickly. Proof, not that Carl had needed any, that people were generally idiots.

He said, "The brothers don't scare me." *And neither do you.* He revealed as much truth as he could. "We're in town at loose ends for a couple of weeks. A contract ran into a snag. Once the paperwork clears we'll be unavailable until the job's done."

With any luck she wouldn't press him for specifics, because he couldn't share any, but the statement had the advantage of being true. The subtext was as clear as he could make it: *Don't get too attached.*

He wondered which one of them he was warning while Felicity sipped her drink, and he watched thoughts flash across her face in profile.

She glanced sidelong at him, warm eyes over a playful smile. That look started with audacity and trust, wrapped it up in desire, and made it breathtaking. "Would this be a good time to confess that I only agreed to help your brother as a way to get into your bed?"

Fear rippled under the bravado. *Hard-hitting offensives*

made quick retreats easier to engineer. Better to hurt sooner than later.

Carl answered with solid eye contact and total honesty. "Would it be a good time to confess that I was desperately hoping he was an excuse?"

Her laugh was even more intoxicating than her smile. "Excellent timing."

CHAPTER 5
AFTERNOON, SATURDAY JULY 11

PARKER LOOKED AT THE lumpy texture of his half-knit scarf and exhaled hard. Felicity tensed up. The man glanced her way, exhaled heavily again, jammed his knitting needles into the wooden tabletop and stalked out of the café.

Not good. Felicity slumped in her seat, feeling defeated.

The metal shafts vibrated, buzzing quietly until Carl wrapped his hand around them and yanked them loose. He sat down in Parker's chair and leaned forward.

He did that a lot: leaned, hunched, or stretched in ways that maximized the open space around himself. Without doing anything overtly obnoxious he'd managed to monopolize the large sofa next to her table right through the busy lunch hour.

"Well, you've certainly been a big help," he remarked to the needles.

That sounded like the facetious prelude to a dismissal. "Oh?"

Carl looked up fast and blinked, the very picture of sincerity. "Oh, yes. There was no breakage this time. Major improvement."

Felicity released tension on a sigh, then laughed when she realized she was doing exactly what Parker had done. "I do like a challenge, but your brother is a handful."

The man had a phenomenal knack for learning by observation, but that was the only educational technique he tolerated. Every attempt to explain a procedure step-by-step was met by sullen grumbling, and he hissed like leaky tire when he was aggravated, which was apparently most of the time.

Carl said, "He's a pain in the ass, but he—" A message alert chirped. "Sorry. That's him." He glanced at the screen on a wristband phone Felicity knew no honest electrician could ever afford, and then he showed the message to her.

I made my target time. Keep your promise. Joining the afternoon mutt session then taking a bridge walk. See you at the lease after sunset if you renege.

Felicity considered the stupid things her brothers found amusing and put two and two together. "What did he win if he lasted longer than the set time?"

Carl leaned back with a smile that raised the temperature of the room. "If he managed two hours without a tantrum, then I had to ask you out for dinner. And breakfast."

The man was astonishing when he grinned like that: all impish humor and sexual heat with a hint of vulnerability that kept charm from turning to arrogance. As if any woman in her right mind would say, *No, thanks, I don't have the appetite for a big hunk of man as delicious as you look. Take yourself away.*

Not leaning over to find out if his lips tasted as good as they looked took more effort than Felicity cared to admit to herself. Then she wondered why she was wasting precious willpower.

Carl met her halfway, and the answer to whether his lips were tasty was *yes.* Yes was followed by *wow* and *holy shit,* and

Felicity's brain didn't start working until after she sat back again.

"Wait," she said as her mind caught up to her libido. "You had to ask me out if you *lost?* Ouch. My ego may never recover."

Too many times in the past she would've felt deeply hurt. Today she could joke because she knew for once she was no one's consolation prize. Carl was making that point abundantly clear.

He didn't actually chuckle; his voice was so deep that it was more like a rumble. "In all honesty it was a win-win for me. If he didn't last two hours then he had to stop harassing me about making a play for you."

"But you'd already—we—"

Felicity lost track of what she was saying, distracted by the intent look in Carl's eyes, so at odds with his casual tone. His smile came up like a rare clear sunrise this time. "It's possible I neglected to mention our conversation in the park to him."

They were still grinning stupidly at each other when Felicity's phone interrupted with her very own note from Parker: *Sorry. Bad fingers, bad temper. I need practice. Can I claim a couple of hours Tues/Thurs after dog training if I bring Carl to referee? Name your price.*

"Oh, look. He's buttering me up for you. How sweet." Felicity decided to delay replying until *Sure, I'll even give you the I-want-to-bone-your-brother discount* stopped feeling like a good idea. "How did he get involved with a therapy dog organization? He doesn't seem like the do-gooder type."

Carl packed Parker's project into its bag before answering. When he did speak the words were slow and thoughtful. "The gory accident—he was on a ward with amputees for a long while.

He saw how the programs helped, he's good with animals. He got hooked."

So very, very careful. Careful was the last thing Felicity wanted. She took a deep breath. "Look, I won't pry, but I cannot keep tiptoeing around the elephant in the room. Let me put it this way: electrician, my ass."

Carl put his elbows on the table and leaned. Hunching. "Half a million women in this city, and I had to hit on one with a cousin in military intelligence."

"Not just any cousin, either. A colonel in the Combined Forces who used to sit on my butt and tickle me when he was ten and I was five." Felicity put a hand over Carl's clenched fists. "He says you're white hats, so that's that. No questions."

Actually her cousin had said, "Thanks for nothing, Flee. Running those names gave my Civilian Security Bureau liaison an aneurysm. They're contract spooks, they shit gold—his words —and they're on a low-risk side job to keep them in funds while they recuperate from getting flattened last time out. Don't pester them."

They'd come to her. It wasn't pestering. She said to Carl, "I feel awkward enough already, so please don't hedge and hesitate. Just change the subject if I hit a sore point. I'm only asking for a little bit of now. A little interlude. Past and future can both go hang."

Carl leaned close and kissed her again. This time he slipped a hand behind Felicity's neck and put enough passion into it to leave her breathless afterwards. Her heart thumped hard in her chest when Carl pressed his forehead to hers and raised his other hand to her cheek.

"No hesitating," he whispered. "And I want a *lot* of now."

The sound sent shivers across Felicity's skin. She tipped her head up just enough to brush her lips against his. "Good."

THE ELEVATOR DOORS CLOSED, and Carl pulled Felicity close; one arm nestled under the weight and warmth of her breasts, the other hand splayed just above the waistband of her pants, under her shirt. "Eighth floor," he said to the sensor.

Felicity lurched against him when the car jerked into motion. Carl bent his head to rub his cheek over her hair. She smelled faintly of cinnamon and felt like heaven. It still wasn't enough to keep him from noticing the walls.

"Are you groping me or using me as a human shield?" Felicity asked.

He shifted his weight. "Both, maybe. I'm a little claustrophobic."

"Nothing about you is little." Felicity wriggled closer, then went still. "Wow, I can feel your heart racing. I'd take that as a compliment except for the sweaty palms. You aren't kidding, are you?"

"No." He inhaled as deeply as he could, breathed out the worst of it. Humor always helped more than sympathy. "No, I'm not."

"There were stairs, weren't there? We could've walked."

"We could've." Felicity liked walking in front of him. The stairs would've put Carl's head on the level of her ass at close range. They never would've made it to the eighth floor. "Walking isn't particularly comfortable at the moment."

Silence fell. Then Felicity offered brightly, "I can help you with that."

"Not here, thanks." Laughter was natural and healthy. How long had it been since he'd laughed so much in one day? *Years.* "I'm also camera-shy."

"Boy, you are one big bag of hang-ups, aren't you?"

Felicity's tone was a tease, and she covered Carl's hands with hers. He responded with the sad truth in a joking tone. "You have no idea."

"Oh, I'm getting the picture." Felicity turned and wrapped her arms around his neck. Then she made a happy little noise in her throat and rose onto her toes. Suddenly the walls were a lot less important than the feel of her breasts rubbing close. Teeth nipped at his neck, and she whispered, "I like a challenge."

The doors eventually released them staggering into the cool, wide corridor. Felicity made another little noise, frustrated and pleased at once, and slid her legs down along the outsides of Carl's thighs to stand on her own. She tilted her hips to press into him the whole way down and nearly brought him to his knees in the process.

Then she laced her fingers into Carl's and swung their hands back and forth as she surveyed the short passage. "Right-o. You have two minutes to get me inside your front door before I start humping your leg. Which door is yours?"

It took him a second to put the words *me* and *inside* back in the right order. *Not in the hall. Not in the hall. Not. In. The. Hall.*

When he picked Felicity up, her squeak of surprise dissolved into giggles that bounced with every step. He palmed the lock plate to open the door, kicked it shut behind him, and set Felicity on her feet so he could get to her clothes. Or his own clothes. *So many decisions.*

He froze at the feel of fingers tugging at his trousers, and

Felicity murmured, "Thirty seconds. Whatever shall we do with the other minute and a half?"

Carl couldn't move for trembling, and he gasped when air hit overheated skin, followed by a firm, exquisite touch. He said, "I won't last even that long if you keep doing—*ah*—that. Stop."

Felicity froze, and Carl cursed inwardly. He'd put too much power into the word, made it a binding command instead of a plea. "Sorry," he whispered. "Sorry."

She shook off the paralysis and looked up. Carl braced himself for the worst, but she hadn't noticed the compulsive force. Her eyes were dancing with amusement and a sweet touch of sympathy.

"Been a while for you too, huh?" She put one hand to her forehead, which made her bangs stand on end in a dark spiky fringe. "I can wait. Bed. We need a bed. We're not horny teenagers. We can get to a bed, right? Where's your bed?"

The way her other hand still clutched at Carl's waistband delivered a clear ultimatum: *Move fast, or I'll be tackling you to the floor instead.*

Carl pointed her in the right direction and followed into his room, which he really should've cleaned up earlier. He threw clothes and dirty towels off the bed and dimmed the lights. Felicity undressed the same way she did everything with her hands; all brisk assurance and understated motions. Coat, boots and socks and trousers were removed and deposited neatly on Carl's desktop before he remembered to breathe.

He sank onto the bed and took a deep breath as she shed the blouse and bra.

Felicity paused. Her lacy briefs glowed pale peach against her skin, and wariness gleamed in her eyes. "You're staring, not stripping. Disappointed by the toy inside the wrapper?"

"Oh, no." She was two-toned in tans and browns in a way that accentuated all the best parts, big and broad enough to hold tight without fear of crushing her. *So gorgeous. So vulnerable.* "More like stunned into immobility."

"Oh." Heat sparked in her gaze again, the shy smile peeked out, and her breasts swayed as she approached. "Do you need help getting started?"

She stopped an arm's-length away. Carl stretched to touch the swell of her hip, over the medical tattoos: vaccinations and contraception were up-to-date. A delicate floral border surrounded the standard dermal applications. *Medicine as art. Marvels of the modern world.* "Beautiful."

Felicity swatted his fingers. "Much too frilly for big, brawny me, but I liked the design. Now show me yours."

Carl shed his coat and got his shirt open before pausing to deliver a reassuring kiss that turned into fondling and the removal of lacy underwear. He was pulling Felicity onto the bed for further explorations when she captured both his wrists and held them firmly.

He quelled his reflexive panic response into a twitch that could be read as surprise. "What's wrong?"

"You are overdressed," she said. "Is this another hang-up? You can't be self-conscious with that magnificent body."

Yes, I could be. Carl turned his hands inside hers and watched puzzlement rise into Felicity's expression as her sensitive fingers caught on uneven skin.

He felt smothered by the deep sudden fear of rejection until he could barely whisper, "Look first. Then say that."

She glanced down at his chest, and tight muscles proclaimed shock and curiosity. *Not revulsion. Not horror.* Carl's anxiety shrank from a suffocating force to a bearable one, and other feelings made a resurgence.

Felicity tugged his shirt off, moved on her knees around him with her hands tapping over thickened bumps and indentations of scar. Goosebumps rose. She combed through his hair, lifted it to see the marks beneath, smoothed her palm down the length of his spine.

Carl watched in the mirror on the closet door and bit the inside of his cheek until he tasted blood. Groaning wouldn't help. It wouldn't do anything except make him wonder afterwards whether he'd pushed too hard for acceptance, created it artificially rather than letting it bloom or wither naturally.

"Did you do this to yourself?" Felicity asked in a resolutely neutral tone. "I know you couldn't possibly reach here—" a tantalizing brush of nails, "—but was it voluntary? I'm not judging, but if it was, then I'm going home to cry into a bottle of wine or two. I am not into pain. Not my scene at all."

He shook his head. Swallowed. "Nor mine."

"You can't imagine how glad that makes me. And sad for you at the same time." Felicity met his eyes in the mirror. "Hurry up, then. Boots. Pants. Off. All of it. Let's see the rest."

Carl complied and sank down again, keeping his focus on Felicity's reflection; it was a lot more attractive than his own. She puffed up her cheeks and blew out a breath that lifted black hair off her forehead.

Then she leaned into Carl's shoulders from behind and slid her hands down his chest, brown and smooth against rough and pale. The sight and the feel of it taxed his self-control past its limits, and all the breath left his lungs on a long, pained moan of frustration.

The woman laughed at him; laughed out loud and without

inhibition: delighted and thrilled to know she could cause that reaction. The sound of it was sweet and hot, and when she spoke again, Carl had to struggle to understand the words. The sensory overload made thought nearly impossible.

"They don't hurt, do they?" she murmured. Her hands skipped over numbed ridges to sensitive areas alongside. "Would it bother you if I—*eep!*"

A moment later she was glaring up at Carl from the bed with a ferocious and wholly insincere frown on her face.

He kissed the tip of her nose. "I got distracted. You were saying?"

"It can wait," she said. Long, warm legs wrapped around Carl's waist. "But you should consider yourself warned. I love playing with patterns."

CHAPTER 6
TUESDAY JULY 28

A SHADOW CROSSED THE doorway to the shop, followed by the chirp of the entry sensor. Felicity looked up from her tatting. "Hi, you. Punctual as always."

Parker dropped his backpack onto the table, then peered warily around the empty shop. His jaw tensed in a now-familiar tic before he said, "No hags?"

His voice was a lighter baritone than Carl's, with a slight drawl that Felicity associated with rural populations. He was getting better about conversation, but he still saved words as if he'd been issued a finite supply and made his points with sound effects when Felicity let him get away with it.

"They left early," she told him. "The growling last week made them nervous."

He took a look into the rear area before returning to the table. The searches were a staple of every visit, as were intimidating hazel glances at other customers and the occasional temper-generated timeout. His enthusiasm and easy smiles made up for a lot, but he was not a restful person.

Felicity put away her tatting and picked up a knitting

project while Parker got his paranoia and his materials sorted out. A huffed-out breath indicated when he was set. Felicity kept her eyes on her rainbow shawl and pretended to not hear.

"Any time you're ready," Parker finally said. "And I'm going to beat Carl to a pulp for asking you to make me talk more. I don't know why he thinks he has any right to be a nanny. He couldn't even take care of hi—*fuck*." He tipped back his head to gaze at the ceiling and hissed for several seconds.

Once he started talking he sometimes went on like that, as if he wasn't sure how to stop. The slips provided insight into why he was so careful about speaking in the first place, and Felicity had been seeing enough of him lately to get used to the oddity of it.

She was seeing even more of Carl. Every afternoon they visited tourist traps in town and across the Bay, and every night found them nesting at Carl's apartment, in part because he had the most decadent bathtub Felicity had ever seen. Miriam was shouldering the extra shop hours without complaint because she could always use the cash, and Abby was jealous.

The self-indulgence wasn't breaking the bank, but the original two-week deadline was long past. The fun couldn't last much longer.

Felicity planned to squeeze the most out of every remaining second of her borrowed time, and that plan included Parker. The tutoring might've started as an excuse, but the man was eager and determined, and Felicity wanted to walk away from this adventure knowing her student would continue to improve if he wanted.

She took her time examining the single-stitch squares he'd produced since the previous Thursday, then lifted one. "You did this one yesterday, didn't you? Everything you knit right after your physical therapy is uneven crap. Does that matter to you?"

Parker's chin jerked up, and he favored Felicity with a hot glare.

Challenge time. Felicity started counting. She'd convinced Carl that sitting in on these sessions was a waste of his time, but his fallback had been to issue pointers like: "If he hasn't blinked by a count of ten, start crying. That'll calm him right down."

Carl was a liar. Tears didn't calm Parker down. They instantly reduced him to stammering mortification. Felicity only resorted to it once. The one-eighty from towering rage to groveling was almost entertaining. *Almost.*

At three seconds Parker rubbed a hand over his face and then scrubbed it back and forth over his barely-there hair. The gesture did nothing to hide the red blush of embarrassment. "Not mocking me."

"I don't mock bad-tempered men with sexy brothers," she assured him. "You know all the basic stitches now, and you can read a pattern like a pro. Do you want to play at this or do it for real? It's a serious question."

"Real," he said after the usual pause. "It's relaxing." He lifted the piece still on his needles. "Mostly. Awful, yes? Also from last night."

Awful would be generous. "You can either rip back the stitches, cut and start over, or live with crap results when you work past exhaustion. You decide."

Parker's quiet laugh caught Felicity by surprise. He set down the knitting needles again, put his face in his hands and his elbows on the table and chuckled to himself through two and a half rows of Felicity's shawl.

She raised eyebrows at him when he discarded the lumpy

work and started over without saying a word. Parker sniffed. Three rows into his new square he lifted it up for review.

Felicity said, "Much better, but I still don't see what's so funny."

He cleared his throat. *Long speech ahead*, that meant. "Carl bitched for months about overwork setting me back. Thought he was full of shit. Naomi's said the same. Didn't believe her either. I couldn't see it." Parker gestured with his needles and a wide satisfied smile. "I *see* this. And I like it."

"Good." Felicity smiled back. "Be careful, though. Knitting is a gateway craft. Before you know it you'll be spinning dog hair and weaving beads. Have you found a pattern to try after you finish the afghan?"

He showed Felicity a ball design which he wanted to try in twine for a cat toy, and they were discussing the adaptation when Miriam and Abby arrived for the day. Customers came and went, there was chatting and flirting, and the rhythms of the shop ebbed and flowed so comfortably around them that the sound of the timer came as a surprise.

Parker set down the knitting and flexed his fingers. "Thursday, yes?"

"Thursday it is," Felicity said as if she wouldn't be seeing him in five or six hours, and she rose from the table when Parker did. This was their routine. She walked him out, Carl met her at the café next door, the two of them spent the afternoon together alone and the evening together with Parker.

Muscles bunched along Parker's jaw. "Not next week."

Felicity felt a pang of sadness. *Nothing lasts forever*, she reminded herself and fended off premature grief with a firm *seize the day, baby*. "Good to know."

As they reached the door, Parker said, "Carl likes you."

"And I like him." *What are we, twelve?* The thought made Felicity smile, and she tipped her face up to the hazy afternoon sun as they left the store. "I'm going to miss both you guys. I wish—"

Parker gripped her arm hard just above the elbow and pulled her around to face him. His growl was a superfluous warning sign. Felicity tried for calm confidence, but her voice shook. "What did I say wrong?"

The look in Parker's eyes wasn't hot temper. It was chilling, and he said, "Do not cling. Warning you. If he ends up more damaged than he is now, I will kill you. He's a hopeless romantic, and he likes you. Do not hurt him."

Felicity fought back the possibly suicidal impulse to say, "What about how hurt I'll feel?" That wasn't the point, and she knew it.

At times there was a bleak weariness in Carl's eyes that made her ache just looking at it. And sometimes, when he thought Felicity was asleep, he sat and watched her. It could have seemed creepy and obsessive except that the tenderness in his expression was so humbling.

They didn't talk past or future because the happy now was as delicate as antique lace. Felicity had no intention of ruining the wonderful memories she'd been creating by yanking too hard on the threads right at the end.

Parker's eyes flicked past Felicity's shoulder to the café.

Carl would be sitting at an outside table with his legs kicked out underneath and his hands cradling a cup of black coffee. He would sit with it balanced on his flat and very muscular belly until it was cold and then he would drink it down in one gulp. That was what he did every day with the same drink, and this conversation was wasting time Felicity would rather spend teasing him about it.

"Romantic?" She went for a light tone to counter Parker's ruthless one. "Are we talking about the same guy? The one who thinks asking 'Sex first or lunch first?' counts as seduction? The one who buys me kitchen implements instead of lingerie? Parker, his idea of pillow talk involves geography lessons. I have socks more romantic than he is."

Parker's expression went from icy to pained, and by the end he was wincing. "He did not buy you cookware."

"He did. I didn't own a stick blender."

It was more romantic than it sounded. Purchase of a phallic motorized toy had led to tons of raunchy jokes as well as useful quantities of whipped cream. Felicity put a hand over Parker's and then turned to slide her arm around him for a sideways hug. "We worked this out at the start. No strings, no clinging."

Carl was waiting right where Felicity had pictured him: big, brooding, and looking washed out in khakis as usual. He pointed a finger at Parker and silently mouthed, "Fuck off."

Felicity sent him a little finger-wave. "Oh, yes, he's a romantic. You heard him. Scram."

Parker gave her a kiss on the cheek that felt like a blessing and then walked away whistling to himself.

THE SOUND OF PARKER'S voice filtered past Carl's bedroom door and woke him from a doze. He listened to the cursing in groggy bemusement, vaguely aware that something was wrong but too comfortable to care. Felicity snuggled closer, her back to his front, soft and bare. Her hand groped until she found Carl's arm and pulled it over her like a blanket. He nuzzled the nape of her neck and started to drift off again.

Felicity was in his bed, and his brother was in the living room. Carl came fully awake with a jolt. When he sat up and turned on the lights, Felicity wrapped both arms around his waist. "S'rong? Bad dream?"

"You could call it that." *Why hadn't the alarm gone off?* Carl snagged his phone and stared at the time on the wristband until it registered. The alarm hadn't gone off because Parker was back from physical therapy over an hour ahead of schedule.

By the time Carl got dressed and closed his door behind him, Parker was slouched back with his feet on the coffee table. Carl sat down on the exercise bench. "You're never home early."

In another worrisome departure from the normal after-session ritual, only one of Parker's arms was draped limp over his belly. The other was propped on the armrest of the couch so he could inspect a pair of panties dangling from one finger.

Oops was what Felicity would've said. Carl clenched his jaw to keep from saying something possessive and confrontational. Parker gave the frilly underwear a long look, glanced at Carl's closed door and then flicked his wrist. The underwear landed on a pair of big wood knitting needles standing in an empty beer bottle. Parker settled deeper into the cushions and smirked.

Carl discarded the first, second, and next dozen comments that came to mind. None of them were remotely rational. Fifteen was: "If you say any of the things you are thinking right now, I swear I will kill you in your sleep tonight."

You could try was Parker's snorted reply. He tilted his head, listened to the sound of Carl's shower running, then heaved himself off the couch. A hand waved—*be right back*—and he ducked inside his room.

Several minutes later, Carl said, "Cough up the news before I choke it out of you with one of your five zillion clumps of yarn."

Parker came out with a duffle in hand and a smile on his face. "They're called skeins, not clumps. I got out early because I have homework."

Two full sentences: the man was practically babbling, and he looked *happy.* Light dawned. "Naomi cleared you for training. Gym or rifle range?"

"Firearms, low power only. Still no contact sports." Parker's brows drew together in a way that indicated his impatience with the restriction. He returned to the couch, picked up one of the knitting needles and began tapping it against the bottle. He was dying to test their potential as hand weapons.

The last of the joy fell away into a scowl when his eyes moved to the closed door again. Regret wasn't an emotion Carl often saw on his brother's face. It took a moment to identify it. Deciphering its cause took another.

"Our approvals came through," he guessed. A month ago he would've been ecstatic. "We got a green light to expand the investigation."

A nod and a sigh. *Sorry.*

"We knew it was coming." Knowing didn't help at all. He wanted more. More time off, more laughter, more everything. The quality of Parker's sympathy told him that he wouldn't even have time to wrap things up gracefully. "When?"

"Need to set taps on the site before midnight to catch end-of-month reports," Parker said. "Eight hours."

Don't waste them moping was the subtext. Carl glared a response that wasn't strictly translatable. Behind him, Felicity said, "Hey, Parker. If you're done playing with my knickers, can you pitch them my way?"

She stood in the bedroom doorway wearing Carl's bathrobe. Her hair was tousled wet, her skin flushed, and the fluffy material covered her from neck to shins, barely hinting at the delightful shape inside. She still looked bold and splendid, and her eyes were twinkling.

It was typical of her to stage a frontal assault on the awkward situation, and the tactic worked brilliantly against Parker. He dropped the knitting needle as if it were red-hot and stood flat-footed and staring.

Carl was torn between enjoying the moment and suppressing an overwhelming desire to punch his brother in the face. Felicity came over to the bench, put her arm around Carl's waist. *Right where she belongs* was the wistful thought that refused to be stamped out.

She said to Parker, "I overheard a little. You'll be back for supper, won't you? Before you both have to disappear at midnight like a pair of Cinderellas?"

One of her many admirable qualities was the easy way she'd accepted that Carl came as part of a set. Parker hefted the duffle and almost smiled. "Three's a crowded pumpkin. You two have a ball without me."

Felicity collected her underwear and sent a questioning look at Carl, making sure she wouldn't disappoint him by insisting. He replied, "No, I don't mind. One last quiet evening together would be wonderful."

He caught his mistake as soon as the words left his lips. *Too late.* Felicity crumpled the panties into a ball and frowned. Parker made an indistinct noise that might have been 'idiot.' Carl ignored it.

"Maybe it's best that we're going our separate ways," Felicity said. "That habit of yours—the one where you answer what I'm thinking and don't wait for me to actually say it first—that could get annoying. Scratch that. It's annoying now. There might be actual knock-down, drag-out fights over it if we kept at this."

The idea caught Carl like a kick to the chest. After a few breathless seconds passed, he saw humor start to melt through the irritation in Felicity's eyes.

She said, "Trying to decide whether to apologize? I mean, you always guess right, but that's not the point."

Carl answered the only way he dared: with blunt, unadorned truth. "I was mourning the lost opportunities for makeup sex after the fights."

Felicity's stunned response made the confession worthwhile,

especially when she flung her arms around him in a laughing hug. Parker took advantage of the distraction to make his escape. His parting gesture was two raised fingers and a grin—*two hours.*

As soon as the door shut, Carl kissed Felicity on the cheek and turned her around to face the bedroom again. "All right, princess. Go say your good-byes to the bathtub while I start on dinner."

"You're cheating again already. I am going to miss that tub." She untied the belt on the robe as she walked away. "Fights, Carl. I'm telling you, we would fight like wet, angry cats."

"I could live with that," he murmured once he was sure she wouldn't hear.

Later, after a simple meal whose preparation involved far too many jokes about blenders for his comfort, they all ended up sitting elbow to elbow on the couch. Felicity worked on something intricate and colorful with a circular, sharply pointed thing she insisted was a knitting needle, and Parker pored over patterns and pointed at things to elicit commentary. The pair of them carried on an arcane conversation about pearls and counting, and Carl sat back and soaked it all in, feeling utterly content and thoroughly depressed at the same time.

When Parker started to fidget and check the time, Felicity packed up her belongings. She gave Carl a wavering smile when he followed her into the hall. "No, don't walk me out. I'm a big girl. I can get home on my own. If there's no more now left, I might as well get a head start on later."

She barely had to stand on tiptoes to reach his lips, and the hug was one last armful of wonderful. Carl didn't want to let go. He wrapped himself around the soft, solid feel of her and said, "Is this a good time to mention that I think that *let's only have now* was a tremendously stupid restriction?"

Felicity pulled back and searched his face. Then she blinked back tears and beamed at him. "Better late than never."

He couldn't promise anything, and he couldn't think of a thing to say that wasn't a promise. Felicity's smile widened, and she put a finger to his lips. "Shush. Don't say it and jinx us. You know where to find me."

"Bossy," he said against the pressure of her fingers. He committed the taste of her skin to memory and found a smile to give back as a farewell gift. "We'll fight."

Felicity bounced as she turned on her heel to leave. "Like angry cats," she said. "I'll look forward to it."

JOINING IN THE ROUND

Less than a month after Carl and Felicity part ways at the end of *Turning the Work,* a single week of violence and terror forever changes the course of their lives. Bombings and riots destroy Felicity's beloved shop and leave her homeless, while Carl nearly loses his life in the fight to stop the criminals behind the violence.

The details of that eventful week from Carl's perspective make up the plot of the novel *Flight Plan.* Carl, Parker, and a band of memorable allies defeat an international conspiracy but almost blow themselves up in the process. Felicity spends that time attending an annual family reunion, safely distant from the drama but devastated by the news of her losses.

Joining in the Round begins a few months later, with Felicity and Carl facing the aftermath of their personal disasters in very different ways.

CHAPTER 1

AFTERNOON, NOVEMBER 21, NEAR ODELL, OREGON

FELICITY CHEN WALKED OUT of the quiet Oregon forest straight into the noisy chaos of her family's autumn retreat week, and the serenity that she'd achieved over the meditative days of her walkabout evaporated like mist. A deep cleansing breath reduced her initial panic to a lump of nervousness she could choke down. She would answer the summons that brought her out of the woods, and then she would leave. Nowhere was it written that she had to stay until the retreat was over. She could face her relatives. She'd survived worse.

Clumps of tents had sprouted in the empty pastures during her month-long absence. Tables and tarps framed outdoor kitchens and sheltered communal dining areas, and the stages were set up with log seats in rows and canopies stretching overhead to ward off the November rains. Split wood was piled high near the raw scar of this year's fire circle, waiting to be built into the bonfire for Last Night.

Everywhere Felicity looked she saw uncles, aunts, cousins, couples and spawn going about the day's activities. The front door to the big log lodge was open, and the broad porch was full of old men and women dozing away the day in their chairs. Flocks of children yelled and laughed and darted around the orchard, throwing as many windfall apples as they collected for cider. Dogs ran yapping alongside them like the watchful shepherds some of them were trained to be.

Six oaks that had been old when the farm was first cleared were dropping their russet leaves on the fading pasture grass. Bare white aspens ranked along the creek, and the last bright foliage of currant and elderberry bushes hid the goat paddocks from view. Shimmers of heat rippled the air over outdoor ovens.

A sweet confusion of voices lifted in song reached Felicity's ears, rising over the steady, distant thump of percussion from the drum circle down near the front gate. Musical practices and performances varied by day and time, but the drumming started as soon as the first guests arrived on Sunday and wouldn't end until the final departures a week later. All the sounds drifted on a cold breeze carrying the scent of spices, wet wool, and grilled foods.

That smell roused a million childhood memories, and a familiar ache set up housekeeping under Felicity's ribs, growing stronger until it pulsed with every heartbeat: always-home-never-home. She could remember the first time she'd felt that swell of melancholy as if it were yesterday. *Twenty years ago, now.*

She was nearing the end of her third decade now, but the pain felt as fresh as ever. She'd spent most of her first revel as a legal adult feeling rejected and worthless, hiding in a back corner of the lodge with her knitting.

She'd been so proud she'd found a way to earn a living and develop her art, but she should've known how her family would react to her news of an apprenticeship two hundred miles away in a field no one respected. She could still remember the snubs and sneers verbatim.

Knitting isn't an art, Flee, it's a hobby. And retail management? What is wrong with you?

Grow up and get a real job.

You want to knit for a living? Are you crazy?

The sneering reactions had crushed her the way only a naïve seventeen-year-old could be crushed. She'd expected her kin to be happy she was following her dreams, but no. They'd mocked and shunned her instead.

By the last night of that revel she'd resolved to never ever *ever* come home again. And she might've gone through with that vow if her uncle Dan hadn't come after her with a guitar and a dose of advice.

Dan was actually a cousin of some degree through marriage, but a ten-year age gap gave him the courtesy title, and patient insistence had gained him entrance to Felicity's sanctuary. She had unloaded her unhappiness on him, and he'd tweaked her nose.

"There's proof of your artist's soul right there, if ever you need it," he'd said. "Eyes full of fire, voice drenched in tears. I will deliver some sage advice, but first let me prove that you're not the first or last feel as you do now."

Then he played a song that expressed how Felicity felt better than her own words ever would. She still hummed the tune when she felt down and remembered Uncle Dan's words.

"Your heart is in your hands," he had said. "Don't listen to fools who can't see the spirit in your craft. You're not alone, love. It only feels so. Some of us understand. Come and dance with us tonight and as often as you can stand it. Don't let bitterness kill all the sweet."

He'd wheedled a promise out of her to visit at least one revel a year, and so she had, every Restoration week in August from then until this year—and this year felt a lot like that one, with her old life falling behind her and the unknown looming large in front.

Poignant nostalgia blossomed into gratitude, and Felicity let it wash away the heavy sense of dread she'd been fighting since August. Her long-ago promise to Dan had likely saved her life. She'd been safe here when disaster destroyed everything she'd built for herself in San Francisco, and she'd not lacked for shelter or support in the wake of her loss.

I can't run and hide forever. Some people respected my grief. It's time to face the rest of them. Felicity settled her backpack and made her way downhill towards the family she could see waiting. After three months mourning her lost future, it was time to hit life head-on again, even when that meant charging straight through the disapproval of her own kin. *Besides, not all of them hate me.*

Her niece Joy greeted her first, from the top of a fence rail. she was treating like a balance beam. Her happy shrieks of "Auntie Flee! Auntie Flee!" attracted the attention of the group collecting apples, and soon Felicity was surrounded by bouncing children and barking dogs. She stayed on course for the lodge. The sea of button noses and beady eyes moved with her, and the chant of "Auntie Flee!" rose and fell like the roar of surf.

Felicity's estrangement from her immediate family was an object warning to many of her peers and elders, but indoctrinating the spawn against the perils of disobedience didn't always work as planned.

To many of the clan's children Flee was the mysterious rebel who lived in far-off San Francisco and only came home for one of the four seasonal revels. They always made a fuss of her. Their happiness at unexpectedly seeing her again so soon was humbling, and their chatter was as entertaining as always.

"Uncle Will says you lost the shirt on your back, but you have a shirt. Whose did you borrow?"

"Did you see bears on your vision quest? We saw a black bear yesterday."

"Will you come on tour now like Auntie Patience and Auntie Charity?"

"I have a new song for my drum! Do you want to hear?"

"Will you help me count the apples I found with only a few bugs?"

The procession broke up between orchard and pasture. Spawn clambered over and under fence rails and carried their excitement past the small cluster of adults approaching from the tent village. Joy worked her way to Felicity against the child-tide and offered a hug. It was like embracing a long bundle of sticks. At the rate the girl was growing she would beat out Felicity for the title of tallest woman in the tall Chen camp, but she was never going to have the heavy bones and broad hips that Felicity had developed along with the height.

Lucky girl, Felicity thought. "You've let your hair grow out since the summer revel."

"Yes, but yours is still longer," Joy said. "And it's straight. I got the frizzy curls. I want to dye it, but Mom won't let me even use henna. It isn't fair. Ben came home on leave from Gov Service all blue."

"He's seventeen. You're twelve. He's also a washed-out Reed. Blue wouldn't suit your complexion at all. Hope is your mother. You have to listen to her." Felicity tousled the girl's hair. All the Chen women had black hair and tawny skin. All of them were notoriously muleheaded too, which made adolescence interesting. Felicity took her role as rebellion-enabler seriously. "But I'll help you try henna, if you have your heart set on it."

"No, thank you. I would have to live through the hysterics after you leave. Hey, Val." Joy scooped up her four-year-old brother as he tottered up to them. "Show Auntie Flee your new whistle."

He put the wrong end of it in his mouth and sucked it contemplatively. Then he announced, "Mommy says you go away with murder. Where are you taking it?"

Felicity smiled over him at Hope and the others, who had stopped a few meters away. "I'll take it far, far away from here, Valiant, just as soon as I can."

His face scrunched up, and tears welled in his eyes. "Far away?"

Oops. Felicity gave Joy a worried look. She was useless with crying children. Joy swung her brother onto a hip with practiced ease. "No worries, Val. She'll always visit family. She loves us. Right, Auntie Flee?"

"Yes, I do. Family matters." Felicity looked past her, across the fence to the rest of her closest family.

Mother had a new pretty boy. So did Hope, Joy's mother. Will's big blonde and Victor's slinky redhead looked familiar, which meant the women might've signed contracts. Felicity tried not to pity them. Only her oldest brother Clement was absent. He always stayed with his husband in the Geary camp. Arlo didn't like Mother much more than Felicity did.

Attack is the best defense. "Hello, Ma. Do not embarrass yourself by offering a space on the Chen site. Everyone knows about the birth-a-baby-or-begone ultimatum, and I will never forgive you even if you did repeal it. Hello, siblings. You've done your duty and come to offer an olive branch. Now go away."

Hope, ever the peacemaker, stayed behind after the others retreated. "Do you have a place to stay?"

"Papa Joe rented me a room in the lodge."

"Good. I'm glad. What are you going to do now, Flee? Do you have any plans?"

Felicity's scalp itched, and her feet ached in her dirty socks. Her clothes stank from days of unwashed wearing. She parried Hope's rude curiosity with honest exasperation. "You mean after I take a shower and do laundry?"

"I mean *next*, Flee. Papa Joe says you've spent half the time since August hiding in the woods. Why come back while the Thanksgiving revel's still going? You hate the parties. Are you looking for money? You ran up a huge comms bill after the news broke."

The debts. That explains all the concern. "Relax, Hope. I don't need a handout. I came in because I got word that the Fed crisis bureaucracy finally coughed up a review of my case."

Felicity's life had literally gone up in smoke, but so had thousands of other lives. All the claims from the terrorist Restoration Plot in San Francisco had overwhelmed insurance and government aid agencies. She'd exhausted herself getting all the necessary filing done before the deadlines, and the hiking expeditions kept her from fretting to death waiting for results.

She added bitterly, "I'll pay Papa Joe and leave as soon as I sign for the settlement funds. There will be no debts. I'll bring no shame to the Chen name, I promise."

That did it. Tears rose in Hope's eyes, and she wrapped her arms around herself rather than reach out to Felicity. "I'm not worried about reputation, Flee. I'm worried about you. Will you have enough to live on? We can help. There are offstage jobs open, and there's the Chen farm. You like animals."

Do not laugh in her face. Don't. She means well. "Hope, the one thing I can guarantee is that I will never work for Oregon Arts and Diversions while Mother is in charge."

She'd turned her back on the family business because she couldn't bear being a second-class citizen. She was too big and ungainly to be a dancer or a tumbler, and she didn't have an actor's memory or a musician's ear.

Production work and public relations provided employment but could never scrub away the stigma of failure. The family farm option was no better. It was a haven for children busy studying and elders too frail to travel, but it was a trap for any adult who didn't want to spend her life serving their needs.

She took Hope's hands and softened bitterness with a smile. "I have some options lined up. I'll let you know my plans once I visit the gatehouse and see how much is in the settlement. Papa Joe might let me get away with murder, but nobody breaks the no-phones rule."

Hope blushed. "I wish Val hadn't heard me say that."

But you aren't sorry you said it. Felicity gave Hope a hug because she appreciated the honesty behind the woman's careful phrasing, and because family did matter. That was the reason the no-phones rule existed.

Retreats and revels were times to focus on matters of the heart and spirit, communal getaways from the everyday world. Other than emergency beacons, no electronics were allowed past the official property entrance on the state highway. Felicity still had a hike before she found out why the security staff had pinged her beacon to bring her home.

She wanted to be clean before she faced that walk, so she headed into the lodge. Papa Joe winked at her from his rocker as she clumped across the porch in her muddy boots. Two of the grannies sniffed, but others smiled.

Ownership of this property passed from each eldest patriarch or matriarch to the next, and it served as a refuge for other elders who had no close kin to care for them. Scandals and melodrama were their favorite forms of entertainment. They liked Felicity because she'd provided a lot of gossip material over the years.

The centerpiece of the lodge interior was a lofted room with an exposed-beam ceiling and walls painted in peaceful earth tones. Upholstered seating groups broke up the expanse of wood floor. Felicity spotted one of her first knitted throws adorning a chair, and a spike of pure pride and love lanced through her as she took the stairs two at a time. She wanted nothing more than freedom now, but there was comfort knowing she would always be welcomed when she came back to this nest.

First she needed to get away. And that meant getting to the gatehouse to find out how far she could afford to fly. She was shucking layers of clothes before she reached her room. The faster she washed and changed, the faster she could be gone.

CHAPTER 2

BY THE TIME FELICITY finished cleaning up, the furniture
in the great room had been pushed into the corners to make
room for a dance practice. She evaded the incoming flood of
cousins and ran downhill through the lower pastures to the gatehouse. A pair of the dogs from the camps tagged along with her,
darting in and out of the brush with waving tails and lolling
tongues.

The drummers outside the tin-roofed log gatehouse had a
small fire going in the center of their circle, and the dancers were
demonstrating the sensual enthusiasm that explained their isolation from the main camp. The dogs peeled off to investigate the
possibilities of petting and treats.

Indoors the twins were working behind the counter in the
security office. Dee Geary kept an eye on the flocks and the
guests by remote camera while Cee sorted through package
deliveries. Both men had coal-black skin, broad cheekbones and
hooked noses, and today they were wearing white poufy shirts
under long brocaded jackets. Head scarves topped off the

costumes, but the modern work boots and wrist comms were distinctly anachronistic touches.

"Doing Peter Pan for the spawn play this year?" Felicity asked.

"Narrr, don'cha know yer classics?" Cee's grin showed off a gold tooth cover. "Treasure Island. Rehearsal after work."

Dee waved. "Hi, Flee. You were on Bald Ridge when I pinged your beacon this morning. Did you sprint the whole way back?"

"I might've rushed a little." Apprehension went sizzling through her. "You're sure it's the case review? Silly question. Of course you're sure. You pinged me." She'd set all her communications to copy forward to the office.

"We're sure." Cee cleared space beside his workstation. "Here, sit down."

"What? No, can't sit. Too nervous." Felicity's hands shook so badly that she had to stop and practice deep breathing again before she could call up her message queue. *Be calm. You can face this.* Her heart soared as she skimmed over the waiting documents. The payment for the shop and apartment would cover the business loan with equity to spare, and salvage sales had added to the total.

Her eyes filled, and her knees went weak. She sank into the chair Cee had maneuvered behind her. He offered a tie-dyed handkerchief. "Is it bad news, then?"

Felicity wiped away the tears and laughed. "No, it's good news. Superb news, even."

She channeled the happiness overload into a concentrated session of calculations, communications, and strategic planning. She didn't have enough money to reopen a new storefront, but if her two employees were willing to work part-time from home then they could keep the brand alive with special orders while she built up capital to invest in a new property.

Dee's voice roused her from her giddy reverie. "Excellent. Here come Laurel and Hardy, right on time. Cee, will you tell them we can finally grant their wish? Flee, you have visitors."

Cee was out of his chair and through the front door in three seconds flat.

"Me?" Bewildered, Felicity went to Dee's desk and took a look at the security monitor over his shoulder.

Two women were waiting patiently beside a utility vehicle parked in the visitor's lot outside the gate. They were dressed like twins in thick gray coats, which was a lot more coverage than the weather warranted unless they'd come from some-place higher in the mountains. Physically they had only stick-straight black hair and pale gold skin in common. One was nearly as tall as Felicity, although far less substantial. She was all narrow bones and lean muscle like a greyhound. The shorter woman had twinkling narrow eyes above high round cheeks, and she was as delicate as a pixie. Together they made quite an eyeful.

Felicity asked, "Why Laurel and Hardy?"

Dee shrugged. "Why not? We have to put something in the log, and they won't give us names. They're also Abbott and Costello, Laverne and Shirley, Lucy and Ethel. This makes day four that they've come asking after you. Do you know them?"

"Never seen them in my life."

Dee sighed in disappointment. Outside, Cee waved the pair toward the gatehouse with a swashbuckling bow. The short one gave him an impish grin in passing. The tall one watched every-thing else with a worried frown and made Cee go first up the walkway.

Dee said, "I can tell you one thing: that one's a CAF discharge with combat trauma issues, or I'll eat my hat."

That comment made Felicity think of another edgy soldier she'd met. He'd had an ambiguous identity and traveled with a mischievous partner too. She'd taught the twitchy one to knit, and the partner had shown Felicity how amazing an ordinary life could look to someone who lived a dangerous one.

Thinking of them, she said, "Did you ask Cousin Henry to run their biometrics past his civvie contacts? He looked up some people for me back in July. I told him there had to be some advantage to having a dirty government bureaucrat in the family."

Dee said, "Of course I asked for his help. He says *dirty government bureaucrat* is passé, by the way. He currently prefers the label *military- industrial sellout*."

Cousin Henry was a lieutenant colonel in charge of regional public relations activities Combined Armed Forces. Felicity wasn't the clan's only prodigal child. She was simply the only one in years who'd gone into trade rather than civil service. Households devoted to the performance arts produced a lot of skillful liars and manipulators. Many clan members ended up fulfilling their citizenship obligations with terms in military or domestic intelligence. Some, like Henry, made a career of it.

The public sector was considered a lesser calling than that of the stage or the studio, but even the rabid antiestablishment zealots on the family tree recognized the value in maintaining ties to the ruling order.

"So, did Henry tell you who they are?" Felicity asked.

"He said they didn't have Bureau files."

"Everyone has files." The government stored biometric identification data on everyone, even foreign tourists.

"Of course, but he can't exactly say they're civilian law enforcers who outrank his liaison or are running under false IDs for official reasons. They say they have news about mutual friends. When did you start socializing with spies, Flee?"

"In July, actually." Fear raised a cold sweat all over Felicity's body and left her mouth dry. "Oh, no. No, no, no."

Her summer lover had been a meticulous, careful man as well as a caring one. No promises, they'd said when they parted, but he might've left instructions to find her.

In case. If the worst happened.

Dee pushed his chair away from the desk and leaned back so he could see Felicity's face. One push of a button locked the front door with a thunk of bolts sliding home. "Do I need to shove you out the back door and swear you were never here? Did you get tangled up in trouble before the Restoration blowup in SanFran last summer?"

I treated myself to a fling and ended up with an undercover agent under my covers. I fell head over heels. He fell off the face of the earth. Is that tangled enough? "It's nothing. No trouble."

Dee's somber stare made her squirm. "There's a story," he said in a threatening tone. He unlocked the door again as Cee and the visitors reached it. "I expect to hear it eventually."

Felicity returned to the reception area. A moment later Cee made a flourishing gesture. "Anonymous mystery women, meet Felicity Chen. Felicity, meet your enigmatic admirers."

He withdrew behind the counter and conspicuously stood listening. Dee joined him. Together they waited with folded arms and watchful eyes. They ignored Felicity's glare. She silently mouthed *Overprotective jerks* at them.

"Very menacing," the short woman said, eyeing them. "I've never been menaced by pirates. I like it."

She had a sweet soprano voice as delicate as the rest of her, and she wasn't acting like someone with bad news. That was hopeful. She stepped forward and stuck out a fragile-looking hand. "Hi there. I'm Naomi Kwan. This is Serena Nguyen. It's good to meet you."

Cee ducked into the office, no doubt to run a background check. Civilians couldn't request a full public records pull on physical data alone, but names were fair game, and biometrics were acceptable for verifications.

Naomi's name sounded vaguely familiar. Felicity searched her memory as they shook hands. "Why are we meeting? I'm told we have mutual friends. Is this about Carl and Parker or whatever their real names are? Did something happen to them?"

"No, no." Naomi flexed her fingers, looking bemused. "They're both fine. Alive. Whatever. Oh, I'm so sorry. Parker should've known you'd jump to conclusions, but he made us promise to meet in person, and maybe I should've left a message, but this is so awkward already—"

"Stop babbling, Naomi." Serena's voice was a brusque alto, every syllable clipped short. "Parker said to lead with this."

Metal glinted between her fingers, and she flung something at the front door. Two long, thin rods hit the wooden jamb one after the other and stuck there quivering.

Serena nodded at them while looking at Felicity. "He says that if you still like a challenge, then you should come home with us and teach Carl the same lesson you taught him."

Her wide, dark eyes were disconcertingly direct. Felicity glanced away. Warm memories of helping a short-tempered man redevelop lost dexterity flickered through her mind. "Parker was always doing that when he got frustrated," she said. "That's where I heard the name Naomi. You were his physical therapist. For his hands."

"I was." Naomi's eyes danced. "And you're the reason he knits doggie boots when he's stressed out. Do you still like a challenge?"

Dee was staring at the door. "Those are *knitting needles?*"

From the safety of the office Cee said, "Yes, and Flee usually has, like, three sets on her. Makes you look at her hobby a little differently, doesn't it?"

"It's a craft, not a hobby—" Felicity said.

Serena spoke over her. "You will help, won't you? Carl is healing with crooked wings, and he snaps and scratches and doesn't listen. You're all feathers and claws and big and solid too. You could make him fly right. Say yes, please?"

That bizarre string of remarks defied response. Naomi cleared her throat to break the silence. "Let me try. Carl got injured, and he's sabotaging his own recovery. Parker thinks you can get through to him. He's away on a job he can't leave, or he'd be here to convince you himself."

"Convince me, or kidnap me?" Parker wasn't the persuasive type. He was more the 'hit things until they cooperate' type.

"Good point. Maybe it's better he's not here. Talking doesn't come easy." Naomi put a hand on Serena's arm. "He isn't the only one with that problem. Sweetie, you could've worked up to the point a little more coherently."

"Sorry." Serena shook her arms and hopped up and down like a fighter before a bout. "I'm trying, but I'm noisy inside, and the pirates are prickly. Outside with heartbeats and hot blood would be better for me."

With that declaration she headed outside, straight across the grassy verge of the parking lot. The dancers were all gone and the drum contingent was down to the minimum two. The lodge bell must have rung for supper.

Naomi moved to follow, then stopped and cast an apologetic look over her shoulder. "I know it's unfair to demand an answer with zero notice, but we wouldn't ask it if wasn't important. This will give you some privacy to decide."

"Go on. I'll think it over." *I've already decided, but you don't need to know that.*

The drummers were tossing a rhythm back and forth. Serena sat down across from them and began clapping out a beat that turned the duet into a trio piece. When Naomi joined them she put one arm around Serena's waist and laid her head on taller woman's shoulder.

Dee and Cee were both frowning at computer screens. Felicity said, "I see why you called those two your daily show. What do their names bring up? Anything I need to worry about?"

The men looked at each other first. Dee said, "Maybe?"

Cee added, "We slammed into Delta-9 security seals. That explains Cousin Henry's warn-away. You're mixed up with people right at the top of the Civilian Security Bureau, Flee. Be careful. Be very careful."

It sounds like Carl needs a swift kick in the ass. Hard to be careful about that. Felicity pictured him as she'd seen him last, with sadness in his deep blue eyes and a smile softening the hard planes of his face. Felicity had warned him they would fight when they met again.

Outside the light was fading and the temperature was decidedly chilly. Both women looked up when Felicity arrived at the drum circle, although Serena kept right on clapping without losing the beat. Felicity found herself the object of the same stare on two different faces. Not similar expressions. Identical ones.

When Naomi blinked, a rosy blush restored individual character to her face. "That didn't take as long as I thought. Have you decided?"

Serena stopped clapping and rose gracefully to her feet. "Crest is up," she said. "Sleek and settled. Choice made."

"You two are seriously weird," Felicity said without thinking.

Naomi burst out laughing. "You don't know the half of it. Does that mean yes? We just got word we need to head home tonight. Can you come with us, or should we arrange for you to follow later?"

Challenging and weird? How can I resist? "I'll come with you." Felicity turned for the trail. "Let's head up to the lodge. You can have some supper while I pack."

CHAPTER 3

EVENING, NOVEMBER 21, NORTHWEST OF LINCOLN, NEBRASKA

CARL'S AXE BIT INTO the log with a heavy, satisfying sound. The impact jolted up his arms, the wood cracked and fell in two separate pieces. He tossed aside the splits. The motion hurt, but pain was more acceptable than either emotional anarchy or the frozen alternative. Anything was better than the numbness.

Even dying? Because if you tear something open doing this, if your lung collapses or you start bleeding inside, then you will die. He shoved aside the bleak thought and paused to toss his jacket onto the half-wall that enclosed the work area on three sides. His body would heal or it wouldn't. He was tired of being careful and hurting anyway.

His breath fogged in front of his face. The sun was going down behind dark clouds on a sweeping flat horizon, and security lights on the neighboring maintenance garage sprang to life as the daylight failed. Uphill across a broad lawn, a three-story rambling farmhouse made a well-lit oasis of civilization in the empty evening. A windbreak of screening trees embraced the building in moving shadows.

He turned his back on it, set the next log in place, and swung. Muscles pulled and stretched, his hand slid along the handle, metal met wood. The repetitive motion slowly created an inner stillness empty of thoughts. He was mid-swing, deep in a peaceful state of meditation, when a hoarse, quiet voice spoke behind him. "Did I plan a bonfire and then forget about it?"

Carl's concentration shattered and the sharp pieces shredded his temper. The axe head hit the stump and sank deep. Rage boiled up, and he fought to keep from wrenching the weapon loose to throw at his unwanted visitor. Blood roared in his ears, and his vision hazed red.

He grasped at one last line of coherent thought: *you do not want to hurt him.* The reminder was a thin defense against the inner bedlam, but it was the only one he had. He repeated the words until he believed them again, then carefully uncurled his fingers from the axe handle and turned. "Hello, Justin."

Justin was sitting on top of the wall, kicking the heels of heavy-soled hiking boots against the bricks. He wore a heavy black coat over a sweatshirt and insulated black pants. The somber outfit was crowned by a jaunty rainbow-hued knit cap, and he wore matching mittens.

The elevation of the wall brought the top of his head above Carl's, which was a reverse of their usual perspective. He met Carl's gaze with steady brown eyes, then lifted both dark eyebrows. The man's face was a portrait in earnest inquiry.

He wasn't oblivious to Carl's reaction; he was indifferent to it. In his mind a sincere question trumped all other factors, even personal peril. His single-minded clarity was always soothing.

Carl said, "You didn't forget a bonfire."

"Well, good."

Silence fell. Carl counted heartbeats waiting for Justin to

think of another way to come at the topic from a tangent. At two hundred Justin asked, "Are you cold? The fuel stove in the house is nice for ambiance and emergencies, but I wouldn't mind if you kicked up the main thermostat."

"Of course you wouldn't. Left to yourself you would keep the place hot enough to fry eggs on the counters." Carl pried the axe loose. "I don't have a good reason, Justin. I felt like chopping wood, that's all."

"Since lunch? I thought I was the obsessive one." Meaning: *All that physical exertion isn't good for you.*

The concern rattled Carl's self-control. "Go away, Justin, or else—" he stopped the words before the ultimatum could take form.

"Or else what? You'll tell me to go jump in a lake? Every body of water for miles is iced over. You'll order me to chop my own leg off with that axe? Did you forget about the impenetrable skin? I guess it might work if you told me to cut slowly. Now I'm really curious. Is that your plan? Or else—what?"

Justin cocked his head to the side. Carl looked long and hard at him. He could make Justin leave. He could make Justin turn around and walk off by saying the right few words in the right voice. The man knew that, and yet he was still pushing. He did not know how to retreat.

Carl held his eyes and said, "Test me. I dare you."

"Nope." Justin shook his head and then slid down the wall to the ground, flexing ankles and knees deep on landing. "I was only teasing. I should know not to do it when we're both in foul moods." He staggered and lurched left. "Ow."

Carl reached out to steady him, then stepped back. "What's wrong?" *Nothing like a distraction to take my mind off my own troubles.* "I thought your ankle fixed itself."

"It did." Justin had smashed his leg to smithereens a few months earlier, but not only was he nearly invulnerable, he also regenerated fast from injuries. He put weight on the leg, wincing. "And the tibia is exactly as mangled as it was when I woke up with superskin. Is healing to a broken baseline irony or paradox? I can never remember the proper definitions."

"Maybe both?" Conversations with Justin quickly drifted far from their original topic. Carl hauled this one back to shore. "If you came outside to cheer me up, you can go back in. I won't hurt myself." *Not today.*

"That was half the reason." Justin's smile fell away. "I also need to warn you I'm heading into a mental bad patch. I meant to collect you after lunch, but I lost the whole afternoon. If the pattern holds, I'll be off-line more often than not for two weeks or so. Tyler's been charting the episodes. I'm definitely on a downward spiral."

He made losing his mind sound like an inconvenience. Sympathy would be the proper response. Carl felt it—felt the pain of it tear at his insides—but he heard himself saying, "You'll be fine. You have a house full of people eager to take care of you while you drool in a corner."

"No, I don't. First you got rid of Parker, and then you scared everyone else into full retreat. It's down to you and me. Great job."

The sarcasm stung like acid, but seclusion *was* a great outcome from Carl's perspective. It was the only way to keep from hurting people when his brain spun out of control the way it was threatening to do right now. He let the remark go unanswered.

Justin sighed. "I always figured Parker would outlast me. What the hell did you say to him anyway?"

The question triggered a memory flash that immersed Carl in one of the worst moments of his life all over again. These days, he had as little control over the full-sensory recall ability as he did over the rest of his reactions. The past swallowed him whole.

His brother's hostile hazel eyes glared into his from three inches away and a few inches down. When Parker snorted, the heat of his breath warmed Carl's throat.

"Leave Naomi alone," Parker said.

"Why should I?" Carl arched an eyebrow, knowing full well it would infuriate the other man. "Is it my fault she thinks I'm more attractive?"

Parker didn't answer with words. He punched Carl in the solar plexus. Breathless pain sent Carl to his knees. His vision sparkled and snowed at the edges before he managed to get air into his lungs again.

Parker waited, hands balling into fists and relaxing, until Carl stopped gasping. Then he said, "You are pulling her strings. You know it, and I know it. Stop."

"Go away, Eddie," Carl said, and he put power into the words. Parker turned on his heel and took two steps before he stopped himself. Carl waited.

In the twenty-plus years since he'd developed the skills to bend others to his will, he had never pulled that trick on his brother. Doing it burned down a bridge he knew could never be rebuilt.

Parker did not even turn around. "Sophocles and Sun Tzu walk into a bar," he said.

There was more to the joke, but Carl had never heard the rest. It was a trigger phrase. By the fourth word, his whole body cramped into a knot of agony. The conditioned response was the most punitive one Parker had ever triggered. Only two were harsher. The worst of them would kill Carl outright, and he'd entrusted Parker with all of them.

He collapsed onto his side and waited, helpless and silent, until Parker relented and recited the countermeasure. His brother knelt beside him. "I don't know why you've thrown your moral compass out the window, and I don't care. The attraction confuses Naomi and drives me crazy. Stop it before I lose control and kill you."

No. I'm trying to keep my lack of control from killing us both. He relied on Parker to rein him in when temptation overwhelmed him, but every time he needed reining in, they danced closer to tragedy. Parker would not let him become a monster, but if forced to that final choice, the guilt would kill him.

Carl would do anything to prevent that, even if it cut out both their hearts in the process. He'd been so sure he could provoke Parker to leave through Naomi. It should have worked ages ago. He bit his tongue hard enough to taste blood. "You've had a dozen job offers. Go, and take her away."

Parker sat back on his heels. "I've tried. I begged. Naomi won't leave while you still need check-ups and physical therapy. And I can't order her to give up. She would ask why. I can't tell her you're fucking with her head. It would destroy her."

Carl's heart sank. He had underestimated the depth of Naomi's drive to nurture and support. She was fearless and tenacious when she felt she was making a difference in someone's life.

No time to dwell on the mistake. He had to find another route to the same end. "What about this: if you leave now, I swear I will stop pulling her heart-strings and convince her to join you. I swear it. You know the promise binds me."

Parker frowned, sensing that he was missing something. Carl

had to keep him from making the connection. "It's a simple choice," he said. "Leave, and know Naomi will be safe from me. Stay, and watch me fuck her brains out, first figuratively and then physically."

And just like that, Carl blinked back to the present, on his knees in wood chips and snow, looking up at Justin's worried face and the darkening winter sky.

"We argued," Carl told him.

"Right." Justin's eyes narrowed, but he let it go. "In any case, you're the only one who can help me until the girls get back from camping."

"What about Tyler? Where's your chief minion?"

"Frolicking with Alison in Seattle, I expect. They are married, after all."

"He knows you're crashing, and he ran off for a conjugal visit? That's callous even by Tyler's standards of insensitivity."

"I sent him, Carl. You ripped him into little shreds of self-loathing over a piece of toast this morning. Yes, he can be annoying as hell, but he's brilliant and he's my friend, and I will not let you push him into slitting his wrists. Who would manage the workshop for me?"

Was I that harsh? Carl wondered. He recalled the confrontation. Tyler had disgusting eating habits, and the man's ego wasn't the strongest. *Yes, I was.*

He knew he should apologize, but what came out of his mouth was anything but sympathetic. "Tyler would never kill himself. He doesn't have the guts for it."

Justin should've slapped him for that remark. Loyalty was one of his foundation personality traits. The man's eyes went cold, his face stiffened, and he got as far as clenching his fists. Then he stepped back and exhaled every bit of the anger.

"It won't work," he said. "I cannot be provoked into abandoning you."

"What makes you think I'm trying?"

Justin snorted. "Expert consultation. I'm told oxygen deprivation after the shooting caused biochemical disruption, and your brain is a finely-tuned weapon. Depression, volatility, and loss of impulse control topped a long list of problems, and isolation was recommended."

The passive presentation meant Justin would not reveal his source. Carl wondered how much money had exchanged hands, and Justin said, "You can have your privacy to wrestle with your demons, but win or lose, I will be there. Count on that."

Justin was impossible to maneuver when he was watching for it, and he did not know how to surrender. Carl sank to his knees, unable to tell if the dizzy wash of emotion that coursed through him was hope or despair. *Both, maybe.* "There's no guarantee this is temporary."

Justin rolled his eyes. "Life is temporary, Carl. I take custody of Ryan at New Year's. I'll find somewhere for you to go if you aren't better by then, or if I'm still drooling in a corner. I won't risk my son's safety."

That it was even a concern—that hurt worse than being punched. "He is in no danger from me, Justin. He never will be. On my life, I promise that."

"Glad to hear it." Justin hesitated. "I'm the more immediate problem. I've sent word to Serena and Naomi, but I will need you to keep an eye on me until they get home."

He knows you're passively suicidal, but he still trusts you with his life. Shame and sorrow swirled up from the void of numbness in Carl's center and lodged in his throat. He swallowed hard. "I will try. And once they're back?"

"Try hard to keep yourself on a leash when I can't run interference for you. Serena won't hesitate to trank you senseless and keep you sedated if you piss her off or make Naomi cry again, but it's a lousy backup plan."

"Institute Admin would've drugged me into a stupor weeks ago. That's standard protocol for situations like this. Slate cleaning, they call it. That's what they meant by full isolation."

"It has a thirty percent cure rate, I hear. "That's storage, not treatment. This is bedder, an'I'll find 'nother way if I haff'a —*shit*."

He stalked off. Fallen leaves on the lawn crunched underfoot. Slurring speech was among the more obvious signs that Justin's brain was shutting down on him. The only thing he hated more than the condition itself was sliding into an episode with anyone watching.

Halfway to the house his progress slowed and stopped. His face was only a blur in the gloom, but the body language was unmistakable. He was lost. The lump of sadness in Carl's throat became a solid ache.

Eight ground-breaking technical patents bore Justin's name. World leaders and corporate titans would still take his calls if he bothered to make any. He could shake off physical damage would kill a normal person. None of that made any difference when he forgot who he was and what he was doing ten meters from his own home.

A whisper of Justin's voice ghosted across Carl's conscience: *try hard. Keep an eye on me.* He grabbed his jacket and went to help.

ACCORDING TO THE TAG on the utility vehicle's rear doors, the car was a rental from all the way out in Pendleton. Felicity slung her pack and her other two bags of belongings into the cargo area to join four empty plastic crates with a local outfitter's name blazoned across the sides. The boxes and the floor were coated in mud and pine needles.

"Were you camping while you waited for me to show up?" Felicity added her tool kit and work bags to the collection. "The wet season isn't fun for most people."

"That's what the guide service told us," Naomi said. "We rented a cabin by Lost Lake. Serena got acquainted with winter, and I learned to drive on ice, so it was win-win. We grew up in San Francisco, and the Plains Territory has been getting buried in snow the last few years." She smiled. "After Mount Hood, Nebraska farm roads should be as easy as pie."

Lincoln, Nebraska, was their final destination. Dee and Cee had the address, and they'd warned Felicity that they would raise hell to Henry if she didn't check in regularly. She settled into the front passenger seat and pulled out her datapad to do some planning. "Are you returning the car to Pendleton and then catching a train, or are you flying out from Portland and taking the penalty fee?"

An impromptu camping expedition hinted at significant disposable income. If they'd flown, then Felicity would have to arrange to meet them at their final destination. She could save for the shop, or she could spend a month's income on airline tickets. She couldn't do both. "Either way I'll need to buy a train ticket, and I can get a cheaper fare if I pick a specific departure time. An ETA would be useful. How far is it to your cabin?"

"What? Oh." Naomi's puzzled frown cleared away to bright amusement that made her eyes sparkle. "We're headed to Pendleton. The service said they'd ship our luggage and pick up their gear later. And your travel expenses are covered. Did you think we'd make you pay your way? That's silly. You're doing us a favor, remember?"

That hadn't fully answered the question, but Felicity let it go. There would be ample time to cover details during the trip. Her estimate of the budget went up another notch, though. Shipping and cleanup services were not cheap.

Naomi glanced out the window. "Are you sure you want to leave tonight? Carl can wait until your reunion is over. I hate to drag you away from all this."

During the hour Felicity spent drying her laundry and packing her few possessions, Naomi and Serena had gotten acquainted with assorted Gearys, Chens, Mendozas, Reeds, and Hunters. They'd been welcomed, of course. Mingling was the whole point of the big free-for-all buffets. People brought their signature dishes and their influential guests to impress everyone else. The drum delegation had stolen Serena away, and Naomi had been conversing about current events with a large circle of admirers when Felicity came to collect her.

"I was on my way out," Felicity said now. "Too much togetherness gets on my nerves. Family, you know?"

"I wish I did, but I'm an only child. I don't usually like crowds, but I don't mind this one. It seems like a nice party." She peered out the windshield. "Maybe *nice* is the wrong word."

The drummers were hammering out a complicated beat while lines of couples stomped and slid and writhed around them. Serena had stripped off the heavy jacket and pants, displaying clingy base layer that clung to her curves. Every spin and twist proved that she was as graceful as she was leggy. Her partner was one of the more talented Mendoza teens—Gillian, if Felicity remembered correctly—and they were mesmerizing to watch.

"Her nickname is Ballerina," Naomi remarked. "She has a lot of energy to work off. You may have noticed she's a little high-strung."

No kidding. Felicity bit the inside of her cheek and kept the words *I cannot wait to find out how Carl met the pair of you* inside where they couldn't offend. "Does she have a nickname for you?"

"She calls me Bao-bao, but we're not lovers if that's what you're hinting. If she makes you uncomfortable, say so, bluntly. She's impossible to insult." Naomi started the motor and revved it. "Unless you call her crazy. Don't do that."

How Serena heard the motor over the drums was a mystery, but there was no doubt she noticed something. Her head snapped around, she stepped out of the dance, and a minute later she was wrapping up a sloppy farewell kiss that left Gilly Mendoza slack-jawed and smiling.

Weird enough to give my bizarre extended family a run for their money. A warm emotion Felicity couldn't quite identify settled over her, soothing away some of her niggling doubts about being too impulsive for her own good.

Serena vaulted over the rail fence into the parking lot, and the truck rocked when she slammed the side door shut and flopped down across the back seat. The small space suddenly filled with the scents of wood smoke, incense, and sweat.

"Fun," she declared as she tossed her outerwear onto the cargo in back. "Fun-fun-fun. Thanks, Felicity Chen. Thanks, Bao. I can be tough like a turtle now."

"Good." Naomi reached out to rest a hand on Felicity's arm. Her smile held a hint of concern. "Last chance to reconsider, renege, or whatever."

"Let's roll," Felicity replied. "I have a million questions. The sooner we hit the road, the sooner I can start pestering you with them."

Serena bounced upright. "No! No nagging. Bao drives quiet. I brought music and homework. Parker says you get homework on all of us. Take this and study first, ask after."

The datapad she handed to Felicity had an unfamiliar brand logo, and the long list of files on it was daunting. Digging through paperwork topped Felicity's list of least favorite activities, but there weren't many other entertainment options. She pulled up a report and dug in.

The information was more than interesting enough to appease her initial irritation. "Homework" meant reading through reams of comprehensive biographical data compiled from sources variously tagged *classified*, *sealed*, and *confidential*.

The first thing Felicity noted was that Carl's name really was Carl, but his surname was Jenson. So was Parker's. They really were brothers, and they were government agents, but only as private contractors. Freelancers specialized in plausibly deniable high-risk operations, so skimming their employment history was hair-raising. Felicity was relieved to learn that they'd officially retired from that line of work.

Other revelations tied off loose ends that Felicity hadn't realized were dangling. In retrospect she supposed she should've guessed that Carl had studied psychology. She'd noticed the irritating knack for predicting reactions. She could forgive herself for not leaping to the conclusion that Carl had specialized in esoteric methods of persuasion and emotional manipulation.

Sometimes learning details hurt more than it helped. Felicity had traced every scar on Carl's body more than once. Learning how the injuries had been inflicted only made her want to cry. When her hands started to shake, she turned to the smaller collection of files on Naomi and Serena.

When she next looked up, grass and scrub were flashing past on either side of the highway at the periphery of the headlights. The navigation screen showed Pendleton coming up fast. A soft instrumental melody was playing on the sound system, and Serena was lying on the rear seat reading from a datapad held overhead at arm's length.

It looked distinctly odd, but Felicity wasn't about to comment. Not after the reading she'd just finished. *Unpredictable* was the third word that came to mind looking at Serena now, right after *exceptionally* and *dangerous*.

Naomi said, "I'm sure you still have a million questions."

"A few." It might be rude to start with, *what's it like to be an honest-to-goodness lab-verified empath when your best friend is a borderline lunatic?* She channeled curiosity into a practical line of inquiry. "Are you managing Carl's physical therapy the way you did Parker's? You said he's sabotaging his own recovery. Is that a professional assessment or a feeling?"

Naomi flashed a glance at her. "You aren't skeptical about the feelings. Not even the teeniest bit."

Have you seen what you look like when you do that? Apparently not, or belief wouldn't surprise you so much. "You may have noticed that my background isn't exactly mainstream. There's plenty of weirdness in the world. Why not empathy?"

"You even know the vocabulary." Naomi's smile made a bright return. "I didn't, not until I fell in with people who think the proper response to anything new is to analyze it to death and then write an article. I am officially impressed."

"Audiences like psychics. Most of my relatives make a living off audiences. The Reeds have an aura-reading act. Most of them carry a rare mutation for increased visual range—they *do* see auras—but they were doing the act for decades before the genes were documented. If you get results, who am I to doubt?"

Serena sat up and hugged the datapad to her chest. "No doubting," she said firmly. "It itches, and I have to keep my clothes on."

"Yes, you do." Naomi shook her head. "I don't need to be psychic to know something is wrong with Carl. It's obvious. He fights everything these days. He does chores he shouldn't be doing yet, he won't do the right exercises, and he's nastier than any client I've ever had, Parker included."

Felicity tried to imagine Carl being nasty. It wasn't easy. The man was two meters tall, but he'd always carried himself with an air of patient gentleness. "So you want me to moderate an intervention?" she asked.

"Basically, yes. It was Parker's idea."

"Then why is he in Australia? Yes, consulting with a security firm, training staff and so on, I read that, but why now? How could he just walk out on his own brother, especially if they're as close as you and Serena are, which is what those reports said." That point had come as an amusing relief. *Finally, an explanation for my inability to* ever *win a game of cards against them.*

Naomi aimed the car at a highway exit. Her lips were pressed tight together as if she was keeping a reply inside. Serena said, "It hurts him, when Carl twists up inside. Cuts him off from safe and makes him not-steady."

"Which means, in English," Naomi said after a short silence, "that I don't handle hostility well, and he was only making things worse. Like a feedback loop. Carl was so *sweet* to me at first, too. Now it's like he's driving us all away on purpose. He even snarls at the boys when they aren't hiding in the workshop."

What boys, and what workshop? Felicity filed that question and all the rest when the truck bumped onto a frontage road and headed for distant runway lights.

Pendleton's regional airfield only saw four or five commercial flights a day. At this hour, the lounge and restaurant in the glass-walled passenger terminal were closed, and the service counter was shuttered. Out on the field a student pilot practiced night landings, and crates were being off-loaded from a cargo plane beside an open hangar.

Felicity waited until they were parked in a vehicle lot beside the terminal building before she accepted that they were stopping here for good. Maybe she hadn't made herself clear on her financial situation. "Is a hotel room covered along with transportation?"

Serena grabbed one of Felicity's bags and snickered as she walked away. Naomi said, "We have a plane waiting."

"You chartered a plane?" *How rich are you?* Felicity grabbed the rest of her luggage and hurried after the other two women, only to stop in her tracks when she rounded the corner of the terminal building.

She'd been picturing a regional puddle jumper: small, sturdy, and low on amenities. The aircraft waiting on the taxiway just past the cargo plane was a shiny white luxury jet—the kind that could seat twenty or more and travel coast-to-coast without refueling. It was the same model the Mendoza cousins used when they went overseas to put on performances for international patrons. Chartering two planes was more economical than commercial tickets for fifty plus cargo.

The economics for three passengers added up a little differently.

A huge flock of butterflies hatched in Felicity's stomach. It was mostly excitement, but there was an element of nervousness as well. Yes, she had a weakness for adventures and mysteries, but this development was enough to put her on edge.

Serena pushed her right into an abyss of uncertainty with one offhand statement. "It isn't a charter. It's my plane. Justin gave it to me."

The butterflies in Felicity's stomach turned to ice and froze every muscle. Disappearing into the night with two obscenely wealthy strangers who had friends in law enforcement wasn't adventurous. It was asking to become a crime statistic.

Naomi came back and laid her hand on Felicity's arm. "Looks like five million more questions just hit you like a box of rocks. If I swear that you're safe with us, will you start breathing again?"

Air came whooshing out of Felicity's lungs on a semi-hysterical laugh, and Naomi beamed at her. "That's better. I know how you feel. Believe me, I know. Hold on a little longer and I will tell you the whole story. I promise."

The plane was as richly appointed on the inside as it was sleek on the outside. Felicity sank gratefully into a bucket seat upholstered in a velvety-soft black suede that invited her hands to stroke it. Serena secured the outer door and disappeared into the cockpit. The engines roared to life a few moments later.

Naomi poured clear liquid into glasses at the bar set into the wall of the cabin, handed one drink to Felicity and sat down in the seat facing her.

"In case you're worried, Serena is not the pilot. She likes watching the ground lights, and I like not being interrupted. Ask anything."

Felicity relaxed and sniffed her glass. It smelled like water. She took a sip and went down her long list to the second question. "Who's Justin?"

"I was afraid you'd start with that." Naomi went back to the bar. "I'm going to need a stronger drink, and you're going to need to sign some legal papers."

CHAPTER 5
MORNING, NOVEMBER 22, RURAL NEBRASKA

EVEN WHEN CARL WOKE up cheerful, the painful necessities of dressing cleared the way for a heavy sense of futility to settle into his bones and pin him down. He couldn't afford to give in, not when had promised Justin help, so when nightmares drove away sleep in the wee hours he tried something different. He skipped all the steps in his morning rituals that hurt and went straight to work.

First he double-checked Justin's preparations. The wall beside every threshold held an electronic display of the simple instructions Justin relied on when his mind was at its worst. The rest of the time the frames held art imagery. Before the sun rose, Carl confirmed the house systems were set with the current messages.

He finished in the kitchen. The wood trestle table at its center gave the place a homey air, and the counters held an extensive collection of appliances. He couldn't recall the last time he'd used any of them. *You liked cooking once. You loved cooking for Felicity.*

For once the message from his inner voice didn't make him

cringe. Felicity meant happiness or luck. He'd been happy, during those few weeks they'd shared. He'd had hopes, before his life fell apart the way it always seemed to do, before picking up all the pieces yet again started to feel like too much effort. Those memories raised a ghost of contentment from its grave, and that inspired him to go through the motions one more time.

The pantry was nearly bare, and dirty dishes were stacked everywhere. Carl improvised with the tools and ingredients on hand and added to the mess before sitting down to sample the results.

The old walls creaked and popped around him as the upper stories warmed in the sun, and it felt as if they were waking up together. The food had more flavor than anything he remembered eating in weeks.

You should do this more often.

He was working on a grocery list when Justin stumbled down the back stairs. The vagueness in his expression wasn't morning drowsiness. His fingers went to the label on the door jamb, tracing the arrow next to the word *Kitchen*. The sign on the door to the yard read: *NO*.

He slumped onto the far bench and stared at his own feet. Grass stains darkened the knees of his jeans, and the thermal shirt was wrinkled, but rumpled untidiness wasn't unusual even when he was at his best. Verbal ability was the key indicator for his mental state, and an easy one to test.

Carl said, "Good morning, Justin. Would you like some coffee?"

Justin squinted. "Coffee."

That's equivocal. Carl said, "Is that yes or no? Are you groggy or off-line? I can't tell."

Blank stare. Off-line, then.

Carl wondered how long he would have to play nursemaid. He clearly wasn't the right person for the job; he hadn't even noticed when Serena and Naomi left. Justin hadn't mentioned where they'd gone, much less when they were getting back.

No point in asking right now. He set a full mug in front of Justin. "Coffee."

The beverage was contemplated with sleepy intensity. Even when Justin's brain was barely working, his innate drive to make sense of his world remained at full throttle. The blend of curiosity and determination could be infinitely charming. Carl felt a smile bubbling up and buried it in a sip from his own cup.

His demonstration was carefully imitated. After finishing the drink, Justin eyed Carl's mostly empty plate. "Eggs," he said.

"Yes, Justin. Eggs." *Also vegetables, cheese, and spices, but if I say omelet I'll probably confuse you. The baked apples and biscuits evidently aren't registering.*

He waited to see where the conversation would go. Justin's eyes went wide, and he triumphantly proclaimed, "Eggs!" Then, while pointing at the apples and biscuits, "Eggs. Eggs. Eggs."

Meaning you want some. "You're the boss." Carl supplied him with food and worked on restoring order to the kitchen while keeping an eye on Justin's progress with his meal.

The man was gnawing on a biscuit when his muscles tightened up and awareness flooded back into his face. He shot a furtive look around the room, stopping mid-chew when he spotted Carl at the sink. Then he started laughing so hard he choked on his food.

Once he got himself under control Carl asked, "What is so funny about clean dishes?"

That set Justin off again. The sound was as joyful as a baby's giggle. Carl leaned against the counter and soaked it up. He could handle a lot of mockery if it brought that much mirth into the world. "What am I missing?"

"First thing I saw—" A vague wave indicated Carl's entirety. "What the fuck is that? I usually feel like a slob next to you, but today you look like you walked out of a video in Serena's erotica collection."

Carl looked down: grease-spattered apron over bare chest and black briefs. Barefoot. Damp hair hanging loose past his shoulders. All that, and he was holding a wet towel.

You are a walking cliché. "I can't decide which is more disturbing: knowing Serena's sexual fantasies lean to domestic role-play or that you've been snooping in her porn stash."

"What, you think she hides it?" Justin swung his left leg onto the bench and rubbed the calf with both hands. "There is middle ground between pin-up and pinstripes. Are you too sore to manage sleeves after yesterday's stupidity?"

Damn the man for being so observant. Carl peeled off the apron and tossed it at him along with the towel. "Maybe I wanted to flaunt my beauty."

"That's a joke right? Hey, you made a joke..." Justin's voice trailed off.

He was looking at the splatter of fresh scarring on the right side of Carl's torso. The largest blotch splashed over older disfigurements like a red spider lying near the center of a pale elaborate web. Carl folded his arms over his chest.

Justin lifted his gaze. "Sorry. I never mean to stare, but the new ones are truly impressive."

"Impressive?" *Not monstrous?* "If you keep coming up with adjectives like that, you can stare all you want."

"Another joke? Shit, Carl, if I'd known that all you needed

was a stint as a caregiver then I would've asked Helen to let Ryan show up early."

"Bad idea." *The last thing I need is a wider target selection. Time to change the subject.* "When will Serena and Naomi get home? Where are they?"

"Playing in the snow somewhere out West." Justin turned his arm to consult a wristband. "Blah, blah sleep, blah, blah errands...later today. They touched down in Lincoln late last night and stayed in town. Why?"

Because I don't know how long I can do this. "Because you and Tyler eat more than a swarm of locusts. There's a provisions order pending on the house account."

"Sure, they can pick it up. Let me find the—there. I've passed it along to Serena." Justin continued checking messages. "They should be here noonish. What are your plans for the morning?"

Crawl back into bed, try to ignore how much my chest, back and shoulders hurt, contemplate my many faults until I'm thoroughly sick of myself. The usual. "Nothing."

"Let's go upstairs." Justin stretched. "I'll get dressed properly and give you a hand getting into sweats and slip-ons, and then you can herd me over to the workshop so I don't wander off and freeze to death on the road."

He left without waiting for agreement. A minute later, Carl finished arguing with himself and followed.

FELICITY SAW MORE shades of brown than she'd ever known existed on the drive from Lincoln to Justin Wyatt's estate. Field after field of withered vegetation displayed endless variations on the theme. Even the overcast sky was closer to buff than slate in tone, and the road was a snaky line of beige though a tapestry of tans, siennas, and umbers. Occasionally the truck passed strips of bare rich soil in shades of mahogany and molasses, and once or twice incongruous bright green grass patches appeared and then fell away the rear.

"It was prettier last month," Naomi said when she noticed Felicity turning to watch a hedgerow full of bare trees. "Snow will help, I hope. Hang on."

"Why—oh!" The road veered sharply left at the top of a gentle rise in elevation that Felicity's San-Francisco-acclimated senses had failed to recognize as a hill.

The pavement was so badly deteriorated that avoiding the potholes was impossible, and they bounced and skidded along for several seconds. Naomi regained control just in time to wrench through another tight curve to the right.

Felicity pushed herself off the door. *No wonder Naomi wanted to practice winter driving.* "Justin Wyatt could afford to pave the whole state if he wanted. He doesn't have a decent road leading to his own home?"

"He's going to repave the whole state, I think. First he's underwriting a mapping project. A lot of local routes haven't been maintained since the Revision years, and they're based on obsolete property lines too. I hope they keep the twisty parts. It keeps the drive interesting even when the view is dull like this."

Felicity looked out again, picturing a pattern with colors alternating like an Icelandic sweater, but in curves instead of sharp zigzags. "It's no worse than fog. I could make a gorgeous blanket using this palette."

Serena leaned forward from the bench seat in the rear of the cab. "Can I help you pick yarn for it? I had fun this morning."

"Me too." *But you were not helpful.*

Naomi had stopped at a store called The Knitter's Nook on the thin excuse that she wanted a gift for Parker. The ruse was abandoned long before a basket of merchandise for Felicity was charged and packed. Remarks like "As long as we're here" and "Justin can afford it" had featured prominently in the conversation.

Felicity hadn't argued much. Handiwork was too important to her peace of mind to live without it even a short while, and she'd finished all but one of the projects she'd brought home over Restoration week. Besides, resistance in the face of Naomi's generosity might have angered Serena.

"I would order wholesale for a large piece," Felicity said now. "And I was thinking of weaving. I would need to pick colors, though, if you'd enjoy looking at catalogues with me."

The offer was sincere, somewhat to her own surprise. Serena had a gift for spotting interesting color combinations that never would've occurred to her.

The suggestion met with a shrug. "Touching is better than seeing."

When Naomi cleared her throat, Serena added, "But thank you for asking."

"You're welcome." Felicity turned back to the landscape. The truck came over one of those deceptive rises and dropped into a cut between grassy hills. Rusting metal posts showed where a fence had once cut across the slopes. A shiny new barrier gate across the road opened automatically as the truck approached.

"Almost there," Naomi said as they approached a cross-roads soon afterwards. "They're in the workshop, right, Serena?"

"The tracker says yes for Justin, but he isn't answering. What about Carl?"

"Feels like he's there too." Naomi made a face. "He's beyond sour now."

Felicity measured the depth of the frown on Naomi's face, and her confidence unraveled. *What if Carl hates being reminded to act like an adult more than he cares about me?*

Failure would not be the end of the world. She would enjoy a day or two in the company of some very interesting people, shake the hand of one of the country's most influential men and leave with a great story to tell at next year's summer revel. *After I drown my sorrows in wine and cry myself to sleep for a few weeks in a row.*

They came to the top of another gentle slope and turned, and the view took her mind off her worries. The ground fell away on one side as if a giant had scooped away the earth, and the road followed the edge of the bluff much too closely for Felicity's peace of mind.

Pale rock walls curved around a flat skirt of bare ground far below, and water in the center reflected the dull sky. Gravel stood in high conical piles near the pond, and deep tire tracks scored the muddy ground. Dump trucks, graders, and other equipment stood idle in no particular order.

They parked beside a metal-sided building near the edge of the cliff. Another utility vehicle was already parked there. A finger-drawn smiley face decorated one dented, mud-spattered door.

The building looked more like a storage shack than a workshop to Felicity. Naomi offered her eyeball and her palm to a biometric reader beside the door, and the panel popped open with a hiss of equalizing air pressure. She stepped aside to let

Serena go first, and the knowing smirk on her face was familiar to anyone with siblings. Felicity schooled her face to neutrality. Naomi got a lot of enjoyment out of springing surprises on people. *We'll see who laughs last.*

The place looked like a storage shed inside too—open rafters, dirty concrete floor, two shovels and a rake stacked in one corner—and it was even smaller than Felicity expected. Serena skipped to the back wall and rapped on it three times. The wall split in the center revealing a small brightly lit room, and she gave the edge of the door a quick affectionate rub as she stepped inside. "Hello, elevator. How are you today?"

The short downward ride gave Felicity time to salvage some composure. When the doors opened again she managed to restrain herself to one undignified squeak.

The cavern was easily thirty meters across. Its ceiling, which was painted blue and white like an Impressionist sky, was brightly illuminated by fixtures set high along the wall. Wiring runs and shiny pipes hung overhead, and conduit snaked down to supply assorted pieces of equipment that Felicity couldn't begin to identify. The floor was grass-green except for an inlaid brick path that spiraled into the mechanical maze.

Yellow brick. *Of course they're yellow. A wizard works here.*

A low hum of electronics and working motors filled the space with a comfortable level of white noise. Warm fresh air wafted past Felicity's face. She turned in a circle to take it all in.

"Workshop, my ass," she said.

Naomi clapped her hands and laughed. "You are hard to rattle. It's incredible, isn't it? My jaw hit the floor the first time. Serena—"

"I hit Justin," Serena said. "But not too hard. Wait until you see the basement under the house. Hot tub, gym, steam room, you name it. They're building a tunnel to here, too, eventually."

"Calling this a workshop is like calling the Pacific a puddle." Felicity's fingers itched to straighten the jumbled wiring runs. Metal access catwalks alongside them were adorned with elaborate decorative detailing. "That's beautiful ironwork."

"Architectural salvage. There's a spiral staircase too, near the center." Serena skipped along the brick path a few steps and came back. "I learned to weld. I should plant flowers next."

"Not today." Naomi turned in the direction of a sudden loud grating noise. "That sounds like our boys."

The brick walkway cut through a series of nooks devoted to specific projects. Between those zones the machines, vats, crates, tubs, and tool racks limited visibility, isolating each work area from the next. Felicity followed Naomi and Serena under an archway of distillation columns and past a corral of gas cylinders. A space opened to their right like a set piece on a carnival ride.

Carl sat atop a workbench with his legs swinging and his shoulders hunched forward. A pair of safety goggles hid his expression. He was watching a short dark-haired man in coveralls kneeling with his back to the aisle.

That would be Justin Wyatt, Felicity assumed. He did something inside a cabinet at floor level that produced a lot of sparks and enough noise to mask the approach of a herd of elephants. Neither man looked up to see their visitors.

Gray was a bad color for Carl. Felicity had told him that a dozen times. His skin was as white as milk, and his hair wasn't much darker. Gray, black, khaki and olive green all made him look faded and ill, but he apparently didn't own clothes in any other shades.

He looks terrible was her unkind first thought, followed by the more exasperated *how does he make a zip-front sweatshirt and sweat pants look formal and tidy?*

The loose material couldn't hide how thin he'd gotten. His nose and brows were sharply defined, his cheeks hollowed. Dark circles beneath his eyes testified to fatigue, and pale beard stubble blurred his upper lip and jaw.

Serena marched into the work zone and slapped Justin on the back of the head. "Phone, crazy man. Why do you have it if you won't answer it?"

Justin lurched to his feet and then tripped over himself turning around. It was a pratfall that any clown would've been proud to perform, only life wasn't a comedy skit, and Justin was holding a power tool with a wicked circular blade. Alarm flooded through Felicity, but Naomi was in the way, and they were both too far back in intervene. All she could do was watch.

Carl came off the lab bench and reached out, and Serena pivoted in time to avoid being gutted. She plucked the tool away from Justin, and Carl got one hand on Justin's collar. He hauled back on that improved handle, spinning Justin into an embrace that should've looked more awkward than it did.

Carl pushed his goggles off, hefted Justin up and turned him to face Serena. "I've got you," he said softly. "Don't panic. Get your feet set."

The tenderness in his voice sent new doubts fizzing along Felicity's nerves. When they'd met she'd mistaken him and Parker for a couple on first and second glance. Carl sent some decidedly mixed signals. Context hadn't helped: men who visited yarn shops in pairs often were couples.

They'd corrected her quickly enough, but now Carl was holding another man as if he were cradling something precious, and the glare he gave Serena was loaded with proprietary anger. Felicity couldn't help but wonder about him all over again.

Serena put her hands on her hips. "Don't you fluff at me, nasty bird. It isn't my fault he goes dark inside."

"No? That slap looked pretty deliberate, and shock is the one thing guaranteed to kick him off-line. He was fine all morning. Now look at him."

Felicity looked.

Justin was broad-shouldered and fit, but he stood only a few centimeters taller than Naomi. Felicity had expected him to be bigger. His face had been all over the news a few years earlier after a plane crash, and more recently too, when the Restoration Plot had spectacularly unraveled at a party he was attending. The dominant impression he'd made was one of sharp, intellectual energy.

His brown eyes looked sleepy and dull today, and he was staring at the power tool in Serena's hand with a puzzled frown pulling at his lips. The expression reminded Felicity of a kitten watching a laser pointer.

This would be one of the "minor neurological issues" outlined in the confidentiality document she'd signed on the plane. *Poor man. No wonder they're so protective.*

Serena said, "I see he's crackling and shifting inside. So what? Dark or bright, he's still spice and quiet. He's still my Justin. Besides, he always brightens up as soon as we get naked and—"

"And make everything worse," Carl said. "Aborting one crash with sensory overload amplifies the next one. Sex isn't the answer for every problem."

"How would you know?" Serena snapped. "Sex isn't your

answer for anything. Why shouldn't we have fun? Don't scratch at me because you're jealous. I will take those claws right off."

Naomi took the cutting tool away from her. "This isn't worth a fight, sweetie. Carl, let him go. We'll take him back to the house. You can join us or sulk here, whichever."

"Look at you, all brave and giving orders." The contemptuous look that came over Carl's face shocked Felicity to the core. His voice was worse. "You think a blade makes you safe from me? I could break you in half before you swung it once."

Naomi whimpered. So did Justin, and Carl reacted with a jerk of muscles and a blink that left him looking merely exhausted again instead of actively malicious.

"Take him," he said as he shoved Justin at the women. "Take him out of here and leave me alone."

That isn't being a stubborn jerk. That is seriously mental. Felicity's stomach knotted up into a painful ball. *What have I gotten myself into?*

Carl hadn't even seen her yet. He was holding his arms tight across his chest and staring at the floor. Serena took Justin's hands and pressed her forehead to his, whispering to him. Naomi stood with her eyes wide and both hands pressed against her mouth.

The silence held for some seconds before Naomi whispered, "What is *wrong* with you?"

Serena transferred Justin's hands to Naomi, then bent to get her face into Carl's field of view, holding herself at a spine-twisting angle as if it were effortless. Her hair hung down beneath her head like a black curtain. "Twisted up worse and worse. Bald spots and broken feathers. Strained wings. Bad bird. *Bad.*"

Carl lifted one hand to rub his forehead. "I don't know what to say to that."

"Don't say anything. Don't fluff. Don't peck and pick and scratch. Stop hurting yourself." She brushed her fingers along his raised arm. "Look who came home with us."

The hammering sound in Felicity's ears was her pulse. Her lungs were empty, but she couldn't breathe in. Carl's eyes were the color of sky after sunset on a clear summer night, and they were utterly devoid of emotion.

"Felicity." He made it sound ugly. Cold.

The chill hardened Felicity's pride. "That's my name. Treat it with respect."

Carl walked away into the maze of machinery without saying another word.

Ouch. The pain of wholesale rejection involved a certain floating sense of detachment. When the dizziness got worse Felicity closed her eyes to hold back tears.

A throat cleared nearby, and then a deep voice that had to be Justin's said, "Well, shit. I missed something important, didn't I?"

Either she bawled her eyes out, or she laughed. It wasn't funny at all, and she didn't mean to be insensitive, but she couldn't help herself. She giggled.

Serena laughed too. That helped.

CHAPTER 6
EVENING, NOVEMBER 22

CARL PACED THE SPIRAL path to the center of Justin's whimsical excuse for a research laboratory and hid there until the others were safely gone. Then he went outside to stretch his legs, only to be reminded that he couldn't escape himself.

The train of thought circling around his brain was driven by the phrase *You are a monster.* Self-recrimination hurtled back and forth past resentful points of interest like *Why can't people leave me alone?*

Motion usually bolstered the illusion of self-control, but the longer he walked today, the more desperate he felt. His path around the property took him off the heights and through creek bottoms lined with bare cottonwoods, but the mire in his mind was worse than the mud he slogged through.

He should've pushed Naomi harder long ago and done whatever it took to send her running after Parker. He would've had to be inhumanly brutal to get past that need-to-help streak of hers, but it would've prevented this catastrophe.

He'd enjoyed knowing Felicity was safe, protected, distant. He'd pretended to believe he might eventually go looking for her the way he'd once wanted. Now that comfort was gone, ripped away by a twist of misguided good intentions.

He couldn't blame Naomi. He couldn't blame Felicity. He could only blame himself, and he had fled because otherwise he would've said horrible unforgivable things.

Coward. If you'd said them, then she would be gone now. She would be safely beyond your reach, but you said nothing. That thought stepped out in front of the express self-recrimination train and derailed it. He'd run instead of lashing out. Why?

Because unlike Naomi, she wouldn't bruise if you hit her with your worst. Felicity could take any punch you throw and turn it back against you. You didn't attack because she might be strong enough to pull you out of this. The idea of living terrifies you. That realization was a stinging slap of insight, and the shock woke up his intellect at long last.

Long shadows stretched out in front of him as he came up the graveled drive to the house and climbed the steps to the front porch. He paused to remove his coat and boots in the mud room off the front hall.

Light shone down the front stairs from the second floor into the parlor and den, gilding the soft fabric tops of chairs and reflecting from lacquered wood tables. Rosy sunset filled the windows, and indicator lights glowed in sleepy readiness along the bottom of the entertainment wall. The formal dining area on the other side of the hall was in full darkness, table and chairs silhouetted in the dim illumination that crept under a service door to the kitchen at the back.

The aroma of browned garlic floated in the air, and voices rose and fell from the rear of the house. Carl's stomach knotted, but he fought down the impulse to retreat into the night and never come back.

He eased open the door at the end of the hall, leaned to peer through the gap into the kitchen. Serena was sandwiched between Justin and Naomi, all of them sitting on one bench with their backs to him. Across from them, Felicity was tapping an empty bowl with a fork.

She was the tallest of the group by a stretch, and she was showing her tough side today in a plaid work shirt and heavy pants. Her dark eyes were pensive, and the corners of her generous mouth were tight with doubts.

Serena had one arm around Naomi's shoulders and the other around Justin's waist. They were listing Justin's way, and he was saying, "Stop stressing about it, Naomi. He always comes in at nightfall."

"And if he doesn't?" Naomi asked. "What if he hurts himself? You don't understand how he feels right now. You can't feel it. You can't know—"

Justin said, "He is not a child. He is clinically depressed, to name the simplest of several serious issues. Hovering over him won't help anyone. And by the way—I know *exactly* what despair feels like, thank you very much."

Silence fell. Wrenching emotional revelations could have that effect on a conversation. Serena turned sideways on the bench, eyeing the hall door. Her frown sent Carl's heart rate soaring. *Busted.*

She only mouthed "bad bird" at him before turning back to Justin. "So, is that why you like morning sex so much? It makes you happy? You're always dark and stormy before we make the bed bounce."

Felicity cleared her throat and got up to clear the table. She was always happier with her hands busy, and she took over the chore so smoothly that no one questioned it. Naomi shook her head, and Justin said in a strained voice, "I adore you, Serena. Leave it at that."

"Okay." Serena's tone broadcast her confusion. "I'm embarrassing you again, aren't I? You don't think morning sex would help Carl? Because I'd be happy to—"

"No." That came from Naomi and Justin both.

Felicity chuckled while she loaded the dishwasher. When she sat down again, the thoughtful frown returned. "He needs professional help."

Hostile resentment rolled over Carl. *You have no idea what I need. You never even knew me. I only showed you what I wanted you to see.*

Honesty whispered back, *You showed her the person you want to be, and she believes in that.* It was a truth that kept him standing there when he wanted very badly to slink away and hide.

Justin said, "The one professional peer we can consult says it's wait-and-hope or nothing, and that we should be thankful he's only depressive and not delusional. The psy-ops programming is nasty shit. You could think of him as a malfunctioning weapon if that helps."

Felicity's expression was priceless. "No," she said. "No, that doesn't help."

Naomi said, "I sincerely apologize for dragging you into this." She elbowed Justin. "I can't believe you kept us in the dark, and I can't believe Parker suggested bringing anyone else into it. I am so mad at him right now."

You aren't the only angry one. Carl touched a diminished presence in his heart, tracing the link that he'd tried hard to sever. The result made him wince.

Dropping Felicity into this was his brother's idea of revenge, a big fat "fuck-you" sent long-distance, wrapped up with a bow and a note that read, "Hurt her like you hurt the rest of us, I dare you."

Felicity said, "Can't he see a regular psychiatrist? What about drugs? There are operations for depression too, aren't there?"

Justin said, "There are limits to physical intervention. Rydder Institute pushes its people right to that edge during development. Find a therapist he wouldn't twist into a pretzel for the fun of it, and I'll pay. Find one useful drug that he could take safely, and I'll buy it. There's nothing...there's..."

Naomi leaned forward. "Justin?"

"He's dark again already." Serena made a disgruntled noise and stood up, hauling Justin bodily along with her like an over-sized teddy bear. "Barely an hour bright. Up we go, crazy man. Bed for you, homework for me. I have to write down times for Tyler. Hey, no biting. I bite back. That's my ear. Quit."

Felicity's mouth dropped open, watching their staggering progress out of Carl's field of view toward the back stairs.

"And I thought my relatives were melodramatic," she said once the footsteps and color commentary receded. "Tragicomedies are so confusing."

Naomi wilted, face and body slumping in defeat. "I can't see the funny side at this point. This was supposed to be a fresh start for us. We were supposed to be happy and together, but it's all gone wrong. I'm so tired of having to be strong and sensible when I feel so alone I want to lie down and cry."

"But you aren't alone. You sensibly came and got me, and I'm glad you did. Honestly. Come here and cry on my shoulder. I can take it."

Felicity knew how to deliver a perfect hug: enough contact

to comfort, not enough to overpower. She let Naomi sniffle for several minutes then released her with a little shake. "That's better. Why don't you go upstairs, take a bath or read a story or do whatever you do to relax, and then call your man and yell at him until he apologizes for not communicating."

"But you—"

"But nothing. Take care of you. I'm self-sufficient. You and Justin both said to make myself at home, so I will. I'm here. I might as well make the most of the experience."

"You mean it? Truly?"

"Truly. You know I mean every word, so don't argue." She coaxed Naomi to the back stairs and shooed her on her way.

Once Felicity was alone she roamed the kitchen as comfortably as if she owned the place. After raiding cabinets for a box of cookies and supplies for making cocoa, she started the stove, put the cookies on the table, and returned to the cabinets. When she collected two mugs, sweat prickled over Carl's skin.

Felicity announced to the room, "I know you're lurking out there, Carl. I can smell you." She set the mugs next to the cookies. "Were you rolling in a landfill all afternoon? Never mind. Come sit with me. I'll feed you."

It wasn't an offer, it was an order. Carl did as he was told.

———

FELICITY SCRAPED the remains of a curry dish Naomi had thawed for supper over the last of the rice from the cooker. The bowl rattled when she set it in front of Carl, and the spoon slipped out of her fingers, clattering onto the table. Her nerves were shot. She might be as stubborn as a mule, but she wasn't stupid. Justin had been serious about describing Carl as a weapon.

Making a fast getaway would be the smart thing to do, but her heart wasn't good at paying attention to her brain. She would hate herself if she walked away from this house full of broken people. She barely knew any of them, not even Carl—*especially not him*—but she never would know more if she left.

Carl hadn't spoken since he walked through the kitchen door with his shoulders slumped and his twilight eyes full of misery. He hadn't even met Felicity's gaze since that first agonized glance. After watching him eat most of the cookies and drink two mugs of cocoa Felicity had risked asking him if he was still hungry. A nod was all the answer he'd offered, so cold leftovers were all he was getting.

He raised one pale eyebrow at the food and sighed. Picked up the spoon and sighed again.

That is annoying already. How soon before I start wanting to slap him every time he does it? Irritation, worry, and pity all frayed Felicity's nerves even further. If she'd known this would happen she would've brought a project bag with her to supper. She folded her hands together and wrapped patience around her other feelings.

Carl looked pathetic, not dangerous. The sweatpants were wet to the knees with muck that had splashed as high as his waist in back. He was barefoot too, and it looked like he was wearing nothing under the sweats.

"Wherever you were, don't go back ever again," Felicity said. "You reek. And please tell me you were wearing shoes at the time, because otherwise I'm dragging you into town for shots and tests."

The threat clearly caught him by surprise. He twitched with

the spoon halfway to his mouth. A bit of the curry fell onto the table with a splat. He set down the utensil with a slow, deliberate motion and sighed. Again.

Felicity grabbed a cleaning wipe before she was tempted to violence. "Am I supposed to guess which tormented adolescent you're playing, or is it more of a generalized archetype?"

That got him to look up. *Finally.*

He had curry sauce on his chin. Felicity wiped his face, sat beside him, and put her hands over his. "The martyred sighs and moody silence. If you aren't playing theater charades, then cut it out. I didn't let your brother sulk, and he was only a client. I'll expect better from you, if you want me to stick around."

And if you speak to me again in that vicious tone you used earlier, she swore silently to herself, *I will walk out the door and never look back. I swear I will.* Her heart whispered, *liar.* Carl said nothing for so long that Felicity wanted to get up and pace and scream. She got up and paced.

"I will do my best to be tolerable," Carl said, and it was his usual deep, gentle baritone. He took a breath, released it *very* slowly, and slid a look up at Felicity before she could snarl at him about it.

His smile sent a thrill through her.

"You missed me," he said.

She couldn't let that pass unchallenged, no matter how phenomenal his eyes were or how promising those lips looked. "Don't get full of yourself. I missed some things. Not the arrogant assumptions."

The eyebrow went up again. "Was I ever wrong?"

Felicity lifted both hands and let them fall to her thighs. "Not the point. I can be right, too. I told you we'd fight, and here we are fighting already."

"Yes, we are." His smile broadened.

The knots of anxiety in Felicity's chest melted away, and she smiled back. She'd warned Carl that they would fight. He'd sidetracked her with the offer of amazing makeup sex.

He stood, swaying on the way up, and Felicity held her breath as he crossed the room. He didn't fall over, which was a relief, but when he leaned in, the air got unpleasantly ripe. Felicity put one hand against his chest and pushed gently. "Not a chance. You need to use a shower and toothbrush before I will consider kissing you."

He leaned a little closer and braced both hands on the counter to either side. "Bossy," he said.

He put an edge on the word, one that cut deep enough to bring all the fear rushing back. The closeness had been intimate. Now it felt like a trap. Felicity swallowed to get some moisture into her mouth. "You like me that way."

"True." When he chuckled, it sounded painful. "All right, you're in charge."

His joints popped audibly when he pushed himself upright, and his progress toward the stairs was pitiably slow. After looking up them, he said, "I might need a little help."

Something in his words brought tears to Felicity's eyes. *You aren't talking about the stairs, are you?*

She blinked away the sadness, put her arm around Carl's waist, and let him rest most of his weight on her shoulder.

"We'll take it one step at a time," she said. "Whenever you're ready."

CHAPTER 7
LATER, NOVEMBER 22

FELICITY WAS WAITING ON the bed when Carl came out of the shower. He stared at her reflection in the mirror while steam wafted through the open door behind him.

His room didn't lack for seating. There was a chaise and a rocking chair as well as seats built into the two window dormers. Felicity had been fully dressed and checking out the amenities when he went in to wash up. Now she wore a pair of loose sheer pants and nothing else, and she was grinning.

The truth sank in: *If you can see her, she can see you. She chose the bed for the view.* Shame flared up. Carl had worked hard to become comfortable in his body, but those gains had been seared and torn away from him one burn, one cut, one ugly degradation at a time. He kicked the bathroom door shut.

"Spoilsport," Felicity called out. "Don't be so shy."

Carl's head throbbed. Resentment seeped past the black fog of apathy to join embarrassment, and temptation rose on the bitter emotional tide. Felicity's cheery poise hid plenty of old emotional scars: *not pretty enough, not clever enough, not sweet enough, not good enough. Never worthy.* Reopening one or all of those wounds would be fair retaliation.

The idea immediately made Carl sick to his stomach, but it still pulled at him. The need to inflict pain was like a yawning pit in the center of the darkness. He closed his eyes and shuddered, teetering on the treacherous edge.

Felicity knocked on the door. "Will you let me brush out your hair if I promise I won't put braids in it this time?"

He remembered the incident—his head, Felicity's lap, a comb, a bout of tickling—and suddenly injured pride and retribution were the last things on his mind. A flood of pure, unadulterated lust washed through him and erased the polluted cravings.

He threw on his robe and opened the door. Felicity was waiting right outside. Her black hair was long enough to tuck behind her ears, and her breasts were on display, brown skin shading paler without tan lines, aureoles rosy-dark around tight nipples. Even barefoot, she hardly had to lift her chin to look Carl straight in the face.

She was blocking the only exit out of a small room. Nothing else mattered. For one awful, wrenching moment Carl felt nothing but panic. His throat went tight, pain flared under his ribs, and he lunged forward.

Felicity *squeaked.*

Carl recovered fast enough to scoop her up instead of shoving her to the floor. The weight taxed his strained shoulder muscles, but he didn't care; Felicity's legs kicked out as he swung her across his chest, and her shriek of surprised laughter nearly deafened him.

She flung both arms around his neck. He got to the bed and concentrated on nipping and licking and tasting. Every caress and touch made the world a little brighter and blew away cobwebs of fear and foul memories.

Felicity was laughing quietly when they came up for air. She kissed his throat and sat up. "Oops. That started with claustrophobia, didn't it? Your big bag of hang-ups is stuffed full these days."

"You have no idea." Respect made him go a step further. He put his feet on the floor and clasped his hands together. *Give her space. Don't push.* "I didn't eavesdrop for long. How much do you know?"

"Enough, Dr. Alan Carl Brown Jenson from Belleville, Ohio." Her shoulder jostled him off-balance. "You slipped and called your brother Eddie once, back in San Francisco. I wondered who you meant. Alan Edward Parker Jenson, right? Both Alans after your father. I would've studied harder if I'd known there would be a quiz."

Unhappiness scraped along beneath the words, residue of some old hurt. Carl resisted the urge to chase after it to the source. "No quiz. I want to be sure you know that I'm..." he paused to repress the words *good for nothing but trouble.* "I'm not entirely sane. I may never be."

One precious memory after another rolled through his mind, carried on the scent of the woman beside him. She smelled like rosemary and mint and a hint of perfume, and every image in his mind was a good one. Carl gritted his teeth. *Please stay. Be my center, take over my heart, be the hot bright fire I need to burn away this darkness.*

Temptation whispered back, *Kiss her again. Seduce her. Make her want nothing more than to stay with you.* The sweet wisp of thought felt nothing like the earlier putrid cruelty, but the lure was just as rotten at its core. He could do it. It would destroy them both if he did.

Felicity cupped a hand against the curve of his cheek, turning him to face her. "Breathe, Carl. Never is a long time." She waited a beat. "Are you feeling sane now?"

No. Yes. Maybe. Carl put his hand on Felicity's thigh. The thin material accented the deep color of her skin, and heat radiated against his palm. Desire stirred again, vivid and clean, and he found the courage to say what he wanted. "You're the best thing that ever happened to me, Felicity. Please don't go."

Felicity leaned back, resting her weight on her elbows. It made her breasts shift in intriguing ways. "I am not a thing, Carl. I'm a great big complicated mess of a human being. I would say *a human being just like you*, but that might make the sex sound a little too weird. There will be sex at some point, won't there? We fought. You promised me sex after fights."

Her petulant tone brought Carl's sense of humor blazing to life. He fell back on the bed and laughed until his stomach hurt. Felicity had a brash appetite for life unlike anyone else he had ever met.

"That's better." She stretched out beside him and propped her head on one hand. Her teeth closed on her lower lip, and she slid her other hand under his robe. "Now take off the armor."

CHAPTER 8
MORNING, NOVEMBER 23

FELICITY TAPPED THE COMB against her palm and frowned at the rumpled sheets on the empty bed. *He was sound asleep. I was only gone a few minutes.*

"Over here."

Carl had retreated to a cushioned built-in window seat. Light from a golden sunrise touched his skin with color. He wasn't a cool blond at all, pale as he was. He would look good wearing crimson. *That, or richer blues and greens. Deep, saturated tones, nothing muted.*

At the moment he wore nothing at all, even though the dormer was open to a frigid draft. He was curled up sideways on the seat, forehead resting against the glass, and he was breathing in deep gulps of fresh air.

They'd made a mess of his hair by rolling around in bed while it was still wet. Even the tangles had tangles. Felicity bit her lip because it would be horrid to say, *you look scrumptious* when Carl was obviously struggling with claustrophobia again. His big bag of hang-ups had a lot of nightmares in it.

"Bad dreams?" she asked.

He shook his head. "Some disorientation on wake-up, but for once no actual nightmares. I slept better than I have in months. I give you credit for that."

That voice of his was like strong red wine: dry, intense, and intoxicating. The effect made Felicity lightheaded, and there was no pretending the cold air was to blame for her shivers. Not when inner muscles were tightening up.

She wanted to lick every spot on Carl's patterned skin, stretch out under the weight and power of his muscles for a while and then roll on top and ride until they were both too exhausted to do anything but sleep the whole day away.

It wasn't going to happen. Fantasy was fine, but she was too sore to make the reality much fun. Even if Carl was up to it. *So to speak.*

The imagination had no limits, but bodies did. Carl currently had a lot of limits. They'd still had quite a night. Felicity burrowed into the piled-up covers on the bed with a warm sense of contentment. *I am well and truly smitten.* "Stop stroking my ego and bring the hair over here."

The window squeaked, sliding shut. Carl unfolded, stretching his legs to the floor, and he tilted his head. He had bruised shadows under his eyes, and his smile looked forced. "Do I have a choice?" he asked.

"Of course, but if you make me chase you, there will be tickling."

He lay on his side, under the sheets and facing away from Felicity, and his shoulders were like a firm, warm wall. She combed out the rat's nests and ran the fine, soft strands through her fingers. *Bliss.*

Daylight slowly brightened the room, and Felicity marveled again at details she'd noted the previous day. The house was full of modern conveniences hidden behind antique fittings.

"I wasn't impressed with this place on first sight," she remarked. "One of the hundred richest men in the world living in a creaky old farmhouse? Very disappointing. Then I saw where the money went. No expense spared on comforts and luxury touches inside and out. I am jealous that you got a bathtub, but my shower's big enough for two. Something to consider for another time."

Carl took his time responding, and when he did, he sounded sleepy and relaxed. "Justin prefers his luxuries simple. Once a country boy, always a country boy, I guess. I'm the same way. I'll take quality over excess any day."

"Simple luxuries. That's a nice phrase. Speaking of nice and Justin—" Felicity squirmed. There would never be a good time to ask. *Better to know sooner than later.* "How close are you two?"

Carl rolled onto his back, which put him at the edge of the bed. "If I respond to the implication, you'll get annoyed by my arrogance," he said. "If I pretend ignorance, you'll get angry about the evasion. I'm doomed."

That wasn't an answer. The distance between them suddenly felt much larger than the width of a body. Felicity poked Carl with the comb. "Talk. You can't distract me. I was raised by magicians and divas."

"And I was raised by people who sanctify lifelong heterosexual monogamy and declare everything else abomination." Carl paused to scrub his hands over his face, pressing his palms against his eyes. "My poor parents. The shame of raising a son who finds men and women equally fuckable nearly killed them both. The monogamy lesson stuck, for what that's worth. I take lovers one at a time, not often, and not Justin. Never him."

Felicity couldn't imagine growing up immersed in rejection like that. She'd only ever faced pity and scorn, not true contempt. "Look, I didn't mean to kick your baggage. Where I come from, it's a courtesy to ask if the coast is clear and to see which way the wind blows, so to speak. Forgive me for misreading things."

She held her breath and waited. Carl kept his face covered. Finally he said, "You didn't misread me, but he's as straight as a ruler."

Felicity let out a sigh. *Ouch.* "Oh."

Carl sighed too. "Yes. Oh. And no. Felicity, you're not a third wheel or a poor substitute or a second choice. Or an alternate. I love you because you are splendidly, uniquely yourself. Never doubt that."

As compliments went, that was one to bring down the house. Felicity waited for the roaring in her ears to subside. "Love?" It came out hoarse. Was she ready for that word? *No, not really. No. Definitely not.*

Carl dropped his arms to the bed and gripped the sheets tight. He kept his eyes shut, but his expression was rueful. "That popped out of nowhere. I didn't mean to frighten you. I claim diminished responsibility. You're naked."

Felicity laughed out loud, relieved to hear that he'd been blindsided by the declaration too. Then it dawned on her that she hadn't said anything about feeling scared—not in words.

She nestled up against Carl, her back to his front, and pulled his arm over her. "You're doing the annoying thing again. How do you cold-read me without even looking? Is it the special psych program you went through?"

"Yes. Rydder Institute calls it neopsych training. People assume it means neopsychology, but it means neo-*psyche*. New brain, roughly." Carl worked his other arm under Felicity's body and enveloped her in warmth. "I process social and emotional cues as unconsciously as seeing colors and hearing sounds. Voice pitch, shifts in weight, scent—the annoying part will only get worse the more time I spend observing you."

His body was quivering. *Warning or promise?* Felicity patted his hand. "Relax, country boy. I can handle you."

"I hope so," Carl said. "The job's open."

The feel of his lips against her neck was incredibly distracting. "What?"

"Never mind," Carl whispered. "It can wait."

CHAPTER 9
LATE MORNING, NOVEMBER 23

FELICITY TOOK A PREP bowl from the drainer, wiped it dry, and then snapped the towel out for the fun of it. It made a pleasing crack of sound, but she realized she should've resisted when Carl flinched. The knife he was washing dropped into the sink, and soapy water cascaded onto the floor.

"Sorry, don't move. I'll get it." Felicity knelt and wiped up the mess. Carl's leg was solid under her free hand. His thigh tensed under the soft fleece trousers as he braced himself on the edge of the counter. Felicity had to exert willpower to keep herself from turning her head and starting the kind of mischief better kept behind closed doors.

Not that the kitchen felt particularly exposed. A casserole was cooking in the oven now, but no one had come to investigate the noise and laughter involved in its preparation. The house felt empty.

Felicity kicked the sodden towel out of the way and stood up, letting her hand slide up to Carl's waist. "Are you still shy about making out in public?"

Somehow she ended up straddling the trestle bench, with

Carl's chest against her back and his face buried in the curve of her shoulder. The novelty of feeling delicate and petite might never wear off.

Carl's legs pressed against hers, and his heartbeat was steady and fast against her spine. "Does that answer your question?" he whispered in her ear.

"No. You could be bluffing. I—hey!" Wet hands slid under the waistband of her jeans and tugged her backwards. *Hello. That is not a bluff.* "Wait, I was teasing."

She felt Carl's chuckle more than heard it. He nuzzled her hair. "Gotcha. I love the way your voice goes squeaky when you get flustered."

There's that word again. "Jerk." She scooted away before temptation got the best of her. "For that, you can finish the cleanup yourself. No using the dishwasher, either. You wanted to handwash everything so you could splash my shirt, and I know it."

Carl made a show of grumbling over the penance, but he hummed while he worked. Felicity took out a project bag and pretended to crochet. Carl had a beautiful voice, and she could listen to him and watch him all day. The way his shoulders flexed when he handled objects with those wide hands, the smiles when he looked at her. *I could get used to all of that.*

"Hi. Can I join you?" Naomi peeked around the corner of the back stairwell.

Felicity beckoned her closer. "Of course! It's your kitchen. Good morning. I wondered where everyone was."

"Justin took Serena out hiking. I slept in." Naomi sent a wary glance at Carl before making herself a quick cup of tea. Carl stopped smiling and stared out the window over the sink. A shiver ran up Felicity's spine.

Naomi sat down at the table and laced her fingers around her mug. She kept her head down so that her hair made a black veil across her face. "Something smells good. Is there enough to share?"

"Plenty. Noodles and cheese go a long way." Felicity kept her eyes on Carl. *What is wrong with him?* "It won't be done for an hour or more. Are you hungry right now?"

"No. I'm not awake yet. I was up all night talking to Parker."

Carl said, "Talking or listening to dead silence? When did my adorable brother start using words?"

His tone was icy, and when he turned, folding his arms over his chest, his scowl was decidedly nasty. Somehow he looked twice as big as he had only a moment earlier. Naomi looked at him like a rabbit watching a snake.

"Since I asked him to try," she said in a tiny voice. "He says he misses me, and he asked me to fly out to Perth to help him assess clients. Since you won't do your PT anyhow, I might as well go where I'm needed."

"Good. Go. I don't need you. Nether does Eddie, to be honest. Nobody needs a spineless cringing mouse. One of these days he'll get himself killed trying to protect you from life."

Tears sprang to Naomi's eyes. "That isn't fair. I never asked for protection, and I got along fine before you people invaded my life. Why are you being so horrible lately? You've been horrible ever since Parker left."

Felicity stood up and put herself between the two of them. For some reason, old advice about bear encounters popped into her mind: stay calm, be human, stand your ground. *He is as big as a bear,* she thought looking at Carl. *A big, thin, extremely grumpy bear.*

"Hi, there," she said. "Have we met? You look just like someone I know who isn't an asshole."

Despite the hostility that rolled off Carl, his blue eyes were glazed and dark. Anguished. "Stay out of this," he said.

"No." Felicity licked her lips. "Apologize. It would serve you right if she does leave, but think of the things we can't do because you get dizzy and your right arm gives out. I'd like you to get back in shape, even if you don't care."

Seconds passed. Carl's hands tightened into fists. Naomi wiped away the tears on her cheeks, gazing at him with worry and at Felicity with awe. Felicity gritted her teeth.

Tremors started in Carl's tense forearms before he said, "Naomi, I am sorry. I don't mean to be horrible to you or anyone else. Please give me another chance."

Naomi pushed back the bench. "Okay, fine. You get one more chance for Flee's sake. I'll be back in an hour for lunch, and I'll give you a session after. If you want backbone, then I'll be the bitchiest therapist you'll ever meet."

As soon as she left, Carl slid down the cabinets to the floor. By the time Felicity reached him he was shaking all over, and his breath hitched in short gasps. She held his hands, and when he relaxed and sighed, she didn't slap him. She squeezed his fingers and brushed back his hair. "What did I just see?"

"When everything is muted, when I get numb, anything seems better, even pain." His face tightened. "Especially pain. I have a lot of cruelty in me, deep down. Naomi puts up a submissive front when she's nervous, and that triggers a nasty automatic reaction. She startled me, and I couldn't stop myself."

Felicity's heart started thumping so hard that she could barely breathe. "That's why Parker isn't here, isn't it? Because you can't always stop."

Another shudder ran through Carl. "I get impulsive. I would've goaded him into homicide, and I—I couldn't do that to him. The guilt would've killed him, if being that close to me when I died didn't do the trick."

Felicity hadn't considered that aspect. *Empathy seems to be tremendously inconvenient.* "So you drove him away to keep him safe," she said. "And you think you're cruel. Speaking of numb, my feet are falling asleep. Can we please sit at the table and chat about life like normal people?"

Carl finally opened his eyes. Amusement lit in them with a welcome blue sparkle. "One of us could."

"I'm not normal. I'm amazing, and don't you forget it."

His smile widened. "Point."

Felicity got coffee started, because caffeine cured ills that even sugar and deep-fried foods couldn't touch, and Carl sat the table with his head in his hands until Felicity set a coffee cup in front of him.

"Eddie has always been there for me," he said once Felicity was sitting beside him. "We've been a matched set since we were five, and he was my anchor, too."

"I would've said you were his anchor, emotionally, but I suppose I didn't see him at his best last summer."

"Or me at my worst." Carl stared into his cup. "Anchor means something specific. Very technical in theory, very simple in practice."

"I'll take the simple version."

"Eddie can shut off my access to the nastier skills that screw with my stability. Not permanently, but even temporary reprieves helped. When he left, I lost that fallback, but—the other risk was just too high."

There was nothing like a fit of histrionics at the dining table to make a place feel like home. Felicity said, "You *really* have to meet my family. You would fit right in. Does the martyr complex come complete with a whip and a big wooden cross to bear?"

Carl pushed aside his coffee and wrapped his arms over his ribs before bending forward to thump his forehead on the table. "It's the depression talking and guilt. Eddie was never supposed to have the caretaker job in the first place. How could I ask him to hold my hand forever?"

I can think of worse fates. Felicity indulged herself by rubbing her fingers over those big broad shoulders. He turned his head to eye her sidelong. Her heart dropped like a rock when she put two and two together.

The job was open, Carl had said earlier. *No, no, no, no. No. I can't be that important to anyone. I can't.*

The casserole bubbled in the oven. Carl thumped his forehead on the table again. Twice. "Stop panicking. I won't ask you. I never even should've hoped."

"Oh, stop it. I didn't say a word." Accepting a snap reaction at face value was unfair under any circumstances. This took unreasonable to orbital heights. Felicity pressed Carl's head down. "And stop that. You will end up with a silly-looking bruise."

"I don't care." His voice was thick with pain, and his skin was damp and hot under Felicity's fingers. "I would rather hurt myself than anyone else. I will not ask. I will not push."

That was a kick in the gut. Felicity gripped Carl's neck harder. "Slow down. I did not turn you down. You deserve a chance to decide if I'm properly qualified for the job, and I deserve a chance to decide if the mind-blowing sex is worth hauling around your baggage. For all you know, you're acting like a baby duck and leaping at the first person to come along."

After a long silence and one of those aggravating sighs, he said, "Bossy."

The knot in Felicity's guts loosened. Sour amusement was better than despair. "Yes, I am. Sit up."

Levering himself upright required pushing off with both hands, and Carl winced. Then he glowered at Felicity. "I am not a baby duck."

She dredged up a matching frown. "No, but you have confessed to impulsiveness. Let's give this a trial run. I promise to boss you around for month or two, until New Year's at the latest. I'll know by then if I want the job, and I'm not staying past then. I don't attend most of my own family's gatherings. I am not crashing Justin's reunion with his son."

"A trial run?" Carl looked intrigued.

"With mind-blowing sex." *Can't hurt to mention that.* "Let me get used to the idea. Give yourself time to see if you hate being given orders. When I'm ready I'll give you a real answer. That's my offer. Take it or leave it."

"You drive a hard bargain, shopkeeper." His smile was the one that made the lines around his eyes crinkle, and it came up slow and strong.

Felicity hesitated. "About the shop. In case no one's told you —" *And why would they?* "It's gone. My apartment too. Between the looting, the fires, and then water damage, the building was a total loss. I got the settlement yesterday, but I have no reason to rush off anywhere. In case you're worried."

Carl regarded her silently, looking stunned by the news. Felicity braced herself. Sympathy made her want to cry, and she was done with crying.

"That's why you jumped at Naomi's offer to come here?" Carl asked. "Free room and board, so you can save money for a new storefront? I'm hurt. Devastated, even. I thought it was all about me and the amazing sex."

Felicity sputtered through incoherent denials until Carl pulled out his grin and said, "Gotcha."

"Jerk."

"Guilty as charged." He started to sigh, but stopped himself when Felicity shook a fist at him. "I'm sorry for your loss. I'll miss that big couch in the back lounge."

"Me, too." Felicity rubbed her hand over his back. "Maybe you can help me pick a new one, when the time comes."

He brightened. "You've got yourself a deal."

CHAPTER 10
MORNING, DECEMBER 5

FELICITY COULD HEAR THE dangerous edge in Carl's tone from halfway up the back stairs. He was always grumpy in the morning, but this was more. She had learned the signs, and he was definitely in attack mode. *I guess lingering in bed to enjoy a little afterglow was a bad idea after all.*

Carl said, "I said fruit bowls, Naomi. Those are soup bowls. Can't you do anything right?"

Naomi said, "Sorry," in her meek-mouse voice.

Carl snorted. "Of course you are."

Teaching Naomi to cook was part of Carl's efforts to bring his nastier reflex reactions under control, but it sounded as if they'd hit a snag. Felicity stopped in the small vestibule between back door and basement stairs and leaned in to see how bad things looked. Interference wouldn't help them learn to work with each other, but neither would letting them fight.

Naomi glanced her way. Her face was flushed, and she looked one blink away from tears. Carl had his back against the counter. Sunlight spilled around his shoulders from the window over the sink, shadowing his face. He said, "You're a sorry excuse for a helper, that's for damned sure. Why does Eddie bother with you? He could do better."

Felicity held her breath. *Come on, Naomi. Slap him down. You can do it.*

Tears ran down Naomi's cheeks, but she straightened up and said, "Fuck yourself, Carl. Nobody asked your opinion."

Her voice shook, but the words did the trick. Carl's shoulders went back as if he'd been physically hit, and he let his arms fall loose. "Dammit. You're right. I apologize. I don't know what set me off. Turn around, will you? Hold your breath. Stop radiating 'hit me' vibes."

He turned around too, staring out the window. Naomi bit her lip and put away the offending crockery. Felicity silently applauded her. *Good job.*

Carl had only slipped like that a few times since she learned to yank hard and fast on the bossiness reins, and he always backed down when challenged. He responded best to direct orders: apologize, back off, take a break, stop moping, shut up and kiss me. Felicity smiled, remembering the aftermath of that particular disagreement.

She'd branched out recently, at his suggestion, to issuing directives: finish your stretches, work your resistance routine, do something useful with your spare time. It lightened the emotional load, he said.

Activity helped lighten his moods too. Felicity had sweet-talked him into helping her put together two week's worth of menus and organizing the pantry to their mutual satisfaction. Then they'd made and frozen most of the entrees, with Serena's enthusiastic if inefficient assistance. Her idea of which foods went together was enough to give a chef nightmares.

Naomi wasn't much better. Her default for any meal was

"cook rice or noodles, make packaged sauce and mix." That led to the idea of teaching her the proper use of Justin's decadent little kitchen.

Now Carl pulled a set of bowls from a shelf far above Naomi's reach and handed them down. "These are the fruit bowls," he said. "I should've been more specific."

Felicity held her breath again. If she breathed, she would giggle. This was serious business wearing absurdity's clothing.

Naomi frowned at the two sets of dishes. "I don't see the point. They're almost the same. Why does anyone need so many different kinds of bowls and plates? It's a waste of time to wash and store and keep track of them all."

"Assigning meaning to—" Carl hesitated. "Do you want a lesson on the sociological importance of ritual and the role of meals in emotional bonding?"

Naomi took the fruit dishes to the table, which was partially set for five places. "No."

"Then the answer is that giving special meaning to certain objects and doing things in certain ways makes people happy."

"Whatever." Naomi looked to Felicity, eyebrows raised. Felicity said, "I can't help. I think you're both right."

Carl turned to look at her.

She wished she could kiss away the pinched, sad lines that crinkled up around his mouth, but public affection was one of the bigger bags in Carl's emotional luggage rack. She settled for a peck on the cheek

"Good morning, grumpy bear," she said. "What's for breakfast?"

He slid both arms around her and bent his head to bury his nose in her damp hair, inhaling deeply as if he could breathe her in. *Better than sighing, I suppose,* Felicity thought, and she squeezed back, trying to send a message: *no one expects perfection. Don't be so hard on yourself.*

Dishes and utensils clinked in the background. Naomi said, "Did I get it all? Frittata—am I saying it right?—is in the oven. Rolls are on the warmer. Fruit is cut and mixed with the goop, and the pots are clean."

Felicity disengaged. "Juice, coffee, tea, and we're set. It smells delicious."

"Thanks. Are we waiting for—" She stopped. "Uh-oh."

Thumping footsteps came down the front stairs, too fast to be anyone but Serena. She came in from the hall carrying a shoe in one hand, and it flew straight at Carl and Felicity the instant she cleared the kitchen doorway.

Felicity ducked. Carl caught the projectile without effort.

"Manners, Serena," he said. "Where are your clothes?"

She wasn't wearing any. Felicity envied the way the woman could wear naked better than some people wore designer dresses. Her fine black hair was loose, waving in all directions, and when she went up and down on her toes, all the parts in the middle rippled or jiggled exactly where they should.

Serena bared her teeth at Carl. "Don't tell me about manners, you selfish, awful, nasty bird. Why can't you be nice to Naomi? You fight, it riles me up, I want to hit things, and Justin's running full dark so he can't help. What am I supposed to do? Do you want me to hit you?"

"No. I don't. And you don't want to try, because that would upset Naomi too."

Also, you would lose, Felicity thought, but that comment was best kept behind closed lips. She sat down next to Naomi, who took her hand and gripped it hard. Naomi said, "No fighting in the kitchen, sweetie. Justin's rule, remember? Clothes *on*, except in the bedroom or the pool."

"I know." Serena's shoulders drooped, her hands flapped, and all the fight went out of her on a breath. "I know, but *oh*. I am itchy and bouncy, and I can't even get Justin to wake up, and it worries at me. Sorry. Sorrysorrysorry."

She sat down and put her head on Naomi's shoulder, and Felicity grabbed the robe that lived on a hook near the back door for her. Once Serena was covered, Carl sat down across from them. He put both elbows on the table and put his head in his hands. Felicity planted her bare foot against his leg: *I'm here. Everything will be fine.*

The timer for the oven went off. A few minutes later, the meal was served, and Serena hummed to herself as she put hot sauce on the fruit. Naomi looked at her, at Carl shoveling eggs into his mouth, and then at Felicity, and she laughed. "I see now. I do! Meals and emotional bonding."

After they finished, Serena filled a plate for Justin and began adding other food and bottles to a carrying tray. "He eats twice as much when he's dark," she said. "And I don't think he'll be bright at all today. Best if I keep him locked in."

Carl said "All day again? We're past the two weeks he said this would last. What are you doing to him?"

"Nothing he doesn't want. He can't help it if the slips are getting longer. Neither can I, so don't you dare blame body-bumping, not when you're getting plenty. Why are you so nasty about him liking me instead of you?"

"I'm a nasty bastard for the same reason you're a crazy bitch. I can't help it. Why are you so sensitive about him? Are you feeling guilty?"

Serena picked up the bottle of hot sauce, and Naomi said,

"Stop it, both of you. Please stop. You're both giving me a headache again, and I have to run errands today."

Carl froze. "Dammit," he said with feeling. "I am hair-triggered today for some reason. Naomi, I am sorry twice now. Serena, please stop stepping on my tail feathers, and I'll try not to ruffle yours. You're right. I was out of line."

"I don't need you to tell me I'm right." She marched off with the tray of food. "You keep your feathers away from my sex life."

"Clothes," Naomi yelled after her. Carl started cleaning up the rest of the dishes, and Naomi sat in a huddle at the table and rubbed her temples.

She wouldn't last a day in the Chen household, poor thing. Felicity considered the potential for continuing drama and decided to take action. "Naomi, the weather report says we're looking at our first big winter storm today or tonight. Maybe you should book a hotel room in Lincoln, just in case."

"There's snow coming? Maybe I should stay home."

Do I have to hit you with my point? "No, you should go now, treat yourself to a nice spa day and a night in town, and then bring the supplies home tomorrow."

"Oh." Naomi brightened up. "What a good idea."

She left to go make arrangements and pack. Carl brought Felicity a fresh mug of coffee. "Thank you for that. She is much better at taking care of other people than caring for herself. I couldn't take the hovering much longer."

The coffee was steaming and heavily sweetened, just the way Felicity liked it. She took her time over it, watching Carl relax as he worked on cleanup. Then a loud buzzer went off, shocking her into spilling hot liquid over her hand.

"Surveyors?" she asked once she recovered.

"Probably." Carl checked the security monitor set into the wall under one of the cabinets. "Definitely."

The survey crews were the only traffic allowed on the private roads. Justin liked hearing about the mapping projects, so the workers had standing orders to stop by whenever they were in the area. Many seemed to consider being in the state close enough. Justin's enthusiasm was as much to blame as his reputation.

"They're going to be disappointed," Carl said. "I'll take care of it."

Felicity licked her hand and tagged along. *This should be interesting.*

The front door opened to a blast of cold air and a trio of hopeful technicians. They declined an offer of coffee when informed that Justin wasn't available, and their disappointment was all but palpable.

Carl delayed their retreat with a question about the day's plans, the answer led to another question, and before Felicity quite knew what had happened, she was pouring coffee and tuning out a conversation about elevations and grades. The happy burr in Carl's voice was all she really cared about hearing.

He's interested in something new. Nice to see, especially when he's having such a bad day. An idea popped up in the wake of that thought, and she caught Carl's eye. He smiled, slow and warm.

Felicity barely had time to think, *Annoying mind-reader* before he turned the smile on the head contractor. "Would you have room for a passenger?" he asked. "I'd love a chance to see your system in action."

They warned him there wasn't much to see, but they were thrilled to include him. Felicity got the impression that opportunities to show off didn't come up often in their profession. She chatted with them about the weather and learned more than she needed to know about their families while Carl dressed for the cold and wet. He looked happier than he had in days as he headed down the drive with them. Felicity sent him a good-bye air kiss from the porch steps, and he lifted a hand in reply.

Later, she had second thoughts and called to check on him. "Tell me you aren't placating them for Justin's sake or humoring me," she said once Carl's smiling image was on the phone screen.

"No." He turned his camera to show dead grass and pavement. *Denying himself input to prove he isn't reading me, not shutting me out.* It didn't make Felicity feel better. He said, "You would only wonder if I was lying. If you can't tell real curiosity from false, then I can't help you. Won't help. And I can't win, because that's exactly what you were hoping I'd say, isn't it?"

Oops. Talk about biting off more than I can chew. "Well, yes," Felicity said. "I had to ask, but I believe you. Can you hear that, too? Look at me. Trust is trust. I trust you. Go play. Have fun out there. I like the idea of welcoming you home."

His chuckle was reward enough. His relieved expression when he raised the phone again was a bonus. "Me too," he said finally, and out came the smile. "I'll look forward to it."

CHAPTER 11
AFTERNOON, DECEMBER 5

FELICITY SET DOWN HER workbag and her wine on the side table and regarded the large lump of striped fur occupying her seat. "That's been my happy spot for weeks now," she said. "Get off."

The tabby cat didn't even look up.

Every day after Felicity finished her business correspondence—filing orders and licenses, scouting real estate—she rewarded herself with a craft break in this particular purple armchair. Her bedroom suite was nice, but this first floor den was a singular delight. A textured fabric partition hid it from the main parlor, recessed lights gave it a warm ambiance, and the jewel-toned color scheme offered a perfect contrast to the wintry vista outside.

A dark line of clouds promised snow to come. Felicity was not about to let a stubborn animal drive her away from her ringside seat at the weather show. She hadn't seen real snow in years, not since moving to San Francisco.

"Off," she said more emphatically.

The tabby yawned, unimpressed. Not one of the six cats

who had house privileges behaved like proper furry lap warmers. They fought with each other, disdained treats, and growled at everyone. Felicity kicked the chair leg. "Scram."

This time she used the tone and the glare that could evict would-be shoplifters from twenty paces. The cat's ears went back, and one paw came up, claws flexed.

Felicity laughed. "Nice try, but you don't stand a chance. Even the big bad intimidation specialist respects me. Last chance, and then I sit on you."

The tabby rolled onto her back instead, squirming into the groove between cushion and arm as if to say, "I respect no one. *I am a cat.*" That cleared enough space for Felicity to sit down, and she did so with a bounce. "I win."

For once the cat neither attacked nor retreated. Instead, she started to purr and leaned softly against Felicity's thigh. "You still aren't a proper cat," Felicity told her. "Not without a name."

She couldn't blame the cats for being jumpy. Serena was in charge of them, and her personality did not make for a restful feline environment. She moved fast and erratically, regularly had loud conversations with inanimate objects, and used the floors as percussion instruments.

The house was quiet. Serena was closeted in Justin's suite upstairs, which brought two thoughts to mind: *thank heavens the walls are soundproofed* and *I should soak up this peace while I can.* She was glad sensitive Naomi was safe in Lincoln. Dinner might get interesting if Serena's temper was still high and Carl's self-control at low ebb, especially if Justin remained off-line. The household tension wasn't likely to improve until he did.

Knitting needles clicked as Felicity pulled her glove-in-progress out of the workbag. "If you're going to be a lap cat, then you need a name," she told the tabby. "What do you think of Mouser?"

Her suggestion was rejected with a blink. Puck, Simba, and Miss Kitty all met with dismissive ear flicks, and Felicity marked out the thumb of the glove. The house speakers serenaded them both with Mozart. Life was perfect until something yanked hard on the slack yarn while she was making increases for the gusset.

A glance over the side of the chair revealed the source of the problem: her workbag was full of calico kitten. Custody was contested fiercely for a few minutes. Felicity won possession of a snarled mess of kitten-plus-yarn ball, and the tabby adult cat stalked away in a huff.

Felicity extricated the hissing kitten from its trap and raised it to eye level. "If you ruined this yarn, I'm making you into ear muffs."

"Is she big enough, or would you need two?"

Felicity dropped the kitten, and it took off like a shot.

Serena was sitting cross-legged on the royal blue loveseat that butted up against the room partition. She wore a red-and-white striped leotard with red leggings and a pink scarf tied around her waist. Her hair was slicked back into a short black ponytail. The outfit should have made her look as innocent as a child, but something about those direct ebony eyes of hers was... disturbing. *Would she really skin a kitten?*

"Where's Justin?" seemed like a safer question.

Serena pointed with her chin. "Right next to you. He likes the yarn too."

The mate to Felicity's chair was the only other seating in the little area, and it was empty. She cut out the ruined yarn section, spliced the pieces and picked up her work. "Right there, you say?"

One section of the legal document she'd signed had contained some patently absurd items. Naomi's warning that certain claims might go unverified during her visit—"Justin's shy about it"—only reinforced Felicity's suspicions. She knew a practical joke setup when she saw one.

Once she had a rhythm going, she said, "I don't see him."

"Of course not. When he's full-dark I keep him boosted to max, so he can't hurt himself unless he falls in a fire or locks himself in a freezer or drowns." Serena raised her arm to show off a wide metallic bracelet. "There's a tracker and controls on my phone. Do you want to see him?"

Conversations with Serena could turn surreal with amazing speed. "Yes," Felicity said, "I would love to see him." *But he isn't really there.*

"Watch for the shimmer." Serena touched the wristband. "Then give him a minute. He says this feels like a kick in the balls. I wouldn't know."

The air next to Felicity's chair rippled like a heat mirage, and then Justin was sitting there on the floor with his nose less than a foot from her arm.

She didn't scream, but she did jab herself with a needle tip. Justin didn't move a muscle. His eyes were squeezed tightly shut, and sweat stood out on his skin. Black hair stuck his forehead in lank, greasy curls, and his face muscles quivered under the heavy beard stubble.

He wore a bright green sweatshirt, red sweatpants, and blue socks with snowflakes on them. *Serena dressed him. I would bet my life on it.* Once Felicity caught her breath she said, "I don't know why you people bother with confidentiality agreements. No one would believe this."

Justin blinked his eyes open and relaxed, and a second later his gaze was locked on the crumpled project in Felicity's lap. If he'd had whiskers, they would've been twitching.

One of the greatest minds in a generation was thoroughly mesmerized by a half-knit glove. Felicity stuck her sore thumb in her mouth to keep from doing something even more inappropriate. *Don't laugh. It's tragic not funny. Do. Not. Laugh.*

Justin tugged on the trailing end of the yarn. Felicity whimpered.

"You can laugh," Serena said. "He likes smiles. Do you mind if we stay here with you?"

"Of course not." Felicity counted the stitches on her needle and got back to work. Justin sat and watched, completely transfixed. Serena brought in the wine bottle and another glass. She also brought a sketchbook, a handful of markers, and a datapad.

Felicity reset her needles to start on the glove fingers. The clouds dropped low, and snow began to fall, blowing along on the gusting wind. Lights came up automatically in the parlor. The soundtrack moved to Bessie Smith and Muddy Waters. Justin lost interest in the knitting and began scribbling.

Sunset arrived behind an eerie orange shroud of snowfall, and Felicity told herself that checking on Carl would be a clingy thing to do. Then she pulled out her handset, only to have it burble at her before she could call.

The two messages carried related news. A weather alert warned that the storm was being upgraded to a blizzard. Carl's note, sent to her, Justin, and Serena, said the road crew was heading for shelter. The storm might interfere with communication, and he didn't want them to worry.

So much for my little fantasy of lying in bed with him listening to the storm outside. Felicity sent a private reply to that effect, then said, "We're on our own tonight. Pizza for supper, then popcorn and a movie?"

Serena nodded. "Finger food is good, but music is better than movies. I need to concentrate on homework."

Her idea of homework seemed to encompass a lot of activities. Felicity decided to risk another dip into surrealism. "What kind of homework are you working on this time?"

"Image and pattern searches. He does that a lot." Serena waved at the artwork in progress "There are ideas. I look for concepts and connections, Justin helps when he's bright, and we pass it all to a team in Seattle for more analysis."

Felicity stretched her mind around the idea of Serena doing pattern analysis while she tried on the glove to check the fit. The lights flickered and failed, casting the room into darkness. Wind gusted so hard that the walls creaked, and snow swirled and scratched against the heavy acrylic window panes.

Cloth rustled, and a draft of air brought the yeasty scent of wine closer. The lights came up again, dim and yellow. Serena was at Justin's side, both hands pressed against his shoulders to keep him seated. She was watching the windows and shifting from foot to foot. Justin was inspecting the carpet.

"Whispery, windy, claws, and cold," Serena said. "Bad. Bad-bad-bad, fight-fight-fight."

That sounds dangerous. "It's only snow, Serena. I saw plenty of blowouts where I grew up. The weather report says this should pass before morning. We'll be fine. How long will the reserve power last?"

"Forever. We have batteries, generators, wind turbines, things." She stopped swaying. "You're right. We are fine. Wise owl. Soft and quiet, big and calm. Thank you. I can do this. Tyler made us a list for storms."

"That was nice of him." *Someday I have to meet this Tyler person and all the other people Serena casually mentions as if I know them.*

Serena tapped her wristband. "There. Now you have the list so you can help me focus." She patted Justin's shoulder. "Up, crazy man. Time for more layers. Tyler says the house cools down."

Felicity tucked away her knitting and brought up Serena's list on her handset. The first item was "Don't panic." Item two was a smiley face next to the words "It's only snow," which made Felicity laugh. Numbers three and four were practical notes related to systems dropping into power-conservation mode. She should shut off unnecessary lights and start the fuel stove located in the dining room for supplemental heat.

Oops. If she'd been thinking ahead, she would've brought in wood earlier. The indoor stack beside the unit was woefully small.

A collection of headlamps hung next to the coats and boots by the kitchen door. Felicity took a light, covered every scrap of skin, and stepped onto the back porch. The wind staggered her, and its icy force blasted through every layer of clothing before she took her first gasping breath. Walking was a struggle, and she kept one hand on the wall or a railing at all times. The world was a circle of snow whirling in the glow of her lamp, and the wood shelter under the porch was already drifted in.

This was the kind of storm that killed sheep and brought down tree limbs in the orchards, the kind that made the elders grumble about moving to the tropics. It was the kind of storm that made anyone with a soul want to shout defiance into the gale. Felicity did, laughing when she couldn't hear her own voice over the howling gale.

Human fears and insecurities seemed petty and unimportant when forces like this were moving in the world. Felicity thought of the decision she'd promised Carl she would give him, the one she kept putting off. It would be easy if he'd asked her to marry him. Marriages were a matter of negotiated terms and time limits. What Carl needed was less tangible and more binding. He wanted to put his life in Felicity's hands.

The idea still shook her to the core when she considered it, but every trip into the cold reminded her of how fragile the present was. She couldn't put off the decision forever. She needed to make up her mind.

No, she realized. *You need to admit to yourself that you've already decided to say 'yes.'*

Once indoors for the last time she stripped off her gloves and pulled out her handset before she even removed her coat. A message would eventually get through, and it was the thought that counted. He'd asked for a promise. When he came back, she would give him one.

For now she sent her heart's whisper over the phone, shaping raw emotion into letters: *Be safe, Carl. Come home safe.* Then she put aside her worries and opened the refrigerator.

This was not a night for pizza. This was a night for using special dishes and making an extra effort.

Blowing snow spun a gauzy veil across Carl's vision. He wiped away the ice building up on his lashes. The light at the intersection between the county highway and Justin's private road was still bravely throwing down a cone of illumination, and the white flakes sparkled as they raced through it.

Drifts were already rising high in some places. Carl leaned against the light pole and hoped the surveyors had gotten to shelter in time. Convincing them to leave had been easy. They'd been soft targets, fatigued after working in the mud and cold all day, distracted by their own plans and concerns. He'd used a smile and a little persuasive force, and they'd gone without question.

The impulse had hit between one heartbeat and the next. He could not even pinpoint why he'd made the decision. He'd been feeling good almost to the very moment when he opened his mouth to say he would stay behind. The exhausting sense of hopelessness abruptly turned to certainty that there was no point to going on.

Enough, he'd thought, and he'd acted.

Better to let a blizzard bury him than to watch the only real friend he had in the world slowly die in stages. Better to let the cold make an end of things than to continue existing as he was now. He couldn't even get through a meal without hurting someone. He was worn down to the bleeding, rotten core by the effort of trying every waking minute. This was for the best.

Your brother will never forgive you for this. None of them will.

Gray apathy smothered that inner whisper the same way it smothered everything else. Second thoughts were pointless. He'd committed to this as soon as he'd compounded the sin of lying to the survey crew by lying to everyone else. Remembering Felicity's cheerful acceptance of the misdirection raised a weak pang of regret. She deserved better.

He should leave her an apology. It wasn't as if he had anything better to do while he waited. When he unzipped his coat to reach his handset, frigid air pushed its way in, and shivers started. His fingers went numb working the case open. Every indicator was in the red. The battery was nearly drained, and the storm was wreaking havoc on reception.

The words wouldn't come. He stared at the screen until he was shaking so hard that his muscles burned from the exertion, but he wrote nothing.

The fluttering signal spiked, and a message arrived. *Be safe. Come home.*

The words slammed through the joyless numbness and shattered it. They were blunt, honest, and demanding, like the woman who'd sent them, and they were all about faith.

Guilt suddenly hurt like nothing else Carl had ever felt, and he'd become an expert on pain over the past decade. The ache swelled up so large that not even the deadened indifference could contain it all, and a fragment of shining wisdom escaped.

Sometimes pain was necessary. He'd been so tired and drained—so *damaged*—that he'd forgotten a critical truth: healing could hurt more than dying. Stitching a wound hurt. Cleaning a burn hurt. So did setting a broken bone. Scars split and bled when they were stretched. Life could be excruciating, but pain was a badge of survival. The same rule applied to the spirit, but that bright truth had slipped away from him and been lost in the fog.

You're an idiot, he told himself and got no argument.

He got up and started walking home.

JUSTIN CAME BACK TO life during supper, going from inattentive to intense on a single breath between mouthfuls of stew. When he sat up straight and cursed, Felicity waved her fork at him. "Hi. Welcome back."

Sometimes Justin laughed when she greeted him that way. Sometimes he was too disoriented to comprehend the words. He remained uncertain of memory and physically unsteady for variable stretches of time after what he called his reboots. *Which will it be this time? Hard or soft?* Either start would eventually end in jokes and curiosity. The man didn't waste a single waking second on bitterness. Felicity had learned that much on the few occasions he'd had been clearheaded long enough to chat.

It was hard to tell whether he was shaky or solid this time; Felicity couldn't see much of his expression or any other part of him. Serena had added layers of black thick fleece over the cheerful colors he'd worn earlier, and the only light came from a collection of candles on the table. Given those factors, Felicity was glad she could tell he was there at all.

Flames licked at wood inside the squat ceramic stove next to him. He had taken his bowl of stew to the corner like a dog with a bone earlier, and he was sitting as close to the heater as he could get without touching it.

"This sucks," he said. His teeth flashed in a grin, and the candlelight caught a glint in the deep brown eyes. "I'm stuck at candlelit meal. When, where, why, and what are all blanks. And if you're wondering, since I'm spilling my guts to you, I also have no idea who you are. Do I know you? Should I scream for help?"

"Please don't scream. You know me, and I'm friendly." *It's only the way he smiles that makes it funny.* After giving him the date and time, she said, "I'm Felicity Chen, if that means anything."

"Not a thing. Keep going, if you don't mind."

"We're at your home in Nebraska. The electrical grid and phone net are both down. Blizzard. There's pepper stew in that bowl and lager in the glass next to your knee. Roasted vegetables and zucchini bread are on the table here. Serena is making dessert, which worries me a little. Does any of that help?"

His eyebrows went up early on, and he nodded in answer to the final question. "That did the trick, yes. Calm, factual, soothing. I see why Carl likes you so much."

"It isn't my serenity he likes." *He has a thing for broad-shouldered brunettes.* "He likes my cooking."

"It smells fantastic." He brought his dishes to the table for a refill. The man had a teenager's appetite, and Felicity wondered where the calories went because they were certainly not padding his wiry body.

While he finished off the rest of the food, Felicity finished off the wine and started tidying up. Justin suddenly said, "Only three plates."

It took a moment to grasp his point. "Naomi is in Lincoln,

and Carl went to ground with a survey crew who came through this morning."

"Shit. Are you sure?" Justin staggered as he stood, bracing a hand against the table. "Dammit. Stupid nervous system. Where did he say he was? What did he tell you exactly?"

Felicity recited the last message to him. Her stomach clenched. Read aloud, the words rang false. Carl hadn't said he was *with* the surveyors, and he was always precise. "Now I'm not sure of anything," she said after she finished.

"He doesn't want us to worry." Justin stared out the dark windows. "Shit. A storm like this, you sit down, you wait, you die. You bastard. That phrasing, the timing—I'll bet anything he's not with the survey crew."

Felicity protested, "But he's been better. I thought he was getting better." *I was so sure of it.*

"Better is dangerous. Better has enough energy to take action when it decides things will only get worse."

Guilt added its weight to Felicity's fear. She should've known that. She should've been more careful, watched him more closely. Common sense responded: maybe so, and maybe Carl shouldn't have lied. Betrayal wove through the other emotions and created tight knots of anger in Felicity's guts. *Oh, Carl, if you live through this, I might kill you myself.*

Serena came through the swinging door from the kitchen with a plate of frosted cupcakes in one hand and three steaming mugs in the other. She frowned. "What's wrong? You're not just bright, you're crackly-sharp."

"Carl is wrong. I need a thing." Justin made a grasping gesture. "Phone. Serena, unlock my phone."

Serena hurriedly slid the plate and mugs onto the table and

dug an earpiece out of the waistband of her leggings. "Say bumblebee seashell."

Justin fiddled with a wristband on his right arm that matched Serena's, then repeated the words while he tucked the earpiece into place. "Voice keys? When did that start?"

"Today. You worked out the numeric code on the bedroom door and ran off while I was napping."

"I did?" The tiny screen on the bracelet lit his face from below, exaggerating his surprised glance. "Interesting. I didn't know I had the brainpower for that when I'm in drool mode."

Felicity felt like a piece of furniture. *Did he hear me mention the phones? Did he forget already?* The angry knots tightened into pain. "What can we do? The wind's going a hundred kilometers an hour out there, drifts are over a meter high, and visibility's zero. Even if we knew where—"

Justin raised one finger and spoke over her. "Hey, it's Justin. Yes, I'm online again. For now. Who's on perimeter tonight? I need them now. It's urgent."

<hr>

AFTER FIVE HUNDRED steps into the teeth of the wind, Carl knew he'd come to his senses too late. He had to lock his knees with every stride because his leg muscles were already weakening. The cold was sucking the life out of him. Clammy sweat trickled down his spine, and he was too tired to even shiver.

He'd made a stupid mistake. Now he was paying for it. *Story of my life. The end.*

The wind whispered in the voices of everyone he'd ever damaged or disappointed, and when moonlight pushed through the racing clouds, ghostly shapes danced through the whirl of shadows.

"Don't get in my way," he told them when he had the breath to spare. "I have to get home." Every so often the lucid thought *you're hallucinating* would bounce through his mind, but he didn't have the energy to hold onto it.

Light sparked ahead of him: a tiny firefly, flickering and indistinct. He ignored it and plodded on. Nothing was real except the icy cold, the pavement under his feet and the need to keep moving.

His boot came down and kept going, pitching him forward into a drift. He sank until the hole was well over a meter deep. Without the constant rush of wind he could hear his own labored breathing and the thud of his pulse.

He rolled onto his back. Light flashed overhead, dazzling bright. A ghost crouched down, and Carl recognized the face behind the goggles. He would never forget those lips.

"Kaylie? Where did you come from? Why are you haunting me? I'm sorry I called your boobs squishy the first time you let me touch them."

"Hiya, Carl." Kaylie tipped her headlamp back. Her hair whipped across her cheeks. Blond stripes alternated with black. Tiger of the month, that pattern meant. She'd outshot and outsparred everyone in the company. "Wouldn't I need to be dead to haunt you? I can't believe you still feel bad about saying my boobs squished. We were what, thirteen?"

"Fourteen. I was stupid."

"True. You were a moron." Kaylie grinned. "A great big handsome moron. I let you kiss those titties after I slapped you, didn't I? Let me give you a hand now."

"A hand?" *Why would I need a hand? I have two already.*

"No, thanks. Go back to shooting anarchists in Borneo or whatever it is you're doing these days. I'm fine resting here."

Kaylie drifted away, and darkness settled again.

If you don't get up, you will die here. He stood up. It took him a while. Wind cut across his face, and hard pellets of snow scraped over the chapped skin. Taking a step resulted in another fall. The snow was warm and soft, and he was tired. Resting felt good.

Light fell around him again in a pool of pure glowing white. There were two hooded figures this time, and a third knelt at his side. "Hey, Doc," it said.

The lights were blinding, but Carl knew the voice. Gruff and confident, it could carry sharp orders through the noise of a firefight one moment and sweetly convince clients to empty their wallets the next.

"Terry?" Carl hadn't seen Kaylie's employer in years, and his conscience came up blank when he consulted it for explanations. He'd always treated her with the utmost respect. Battle-hardened soldiers hesitated to anger the woman. She ran her security firm with a hard head and a fair hand. "What did I ever do to you?"

"We don't have time for the whole list. Listen up, Doc. We are under explicit orders. No interference except to keep you quarantined. If you're ready to cash out, you get that option. Our hands are tied."

Why the obsession with hands? Carl looked. "No, they're not."

"Goddamn, your brain is frozen." Terry grabbed Carl's coat collar in both hands and shook him. "The mumbling doesn't cut it. Give me a straight answer. Do you want to live or die? Yes or no."

That was unfair. Which was which? "I want to go home, but I'm all turned around, and I'm tired. I don't know which way the farm is."

"Good enough for me. Up you go." Terry tightened her grip and hauled Carl to his feet.

Sound rumbled nearby. Carl made sense of the noise when he saw the tracks in the snow, but comprehension only left him puzzling over the question, *Why do ghosts need snowmobiles?*

A little later, inside a warm office with a mug of hot coffee in his hands and heat packs under his arms, he was glad he hadn't asked the question out loud.

JUSTIN LIMPED around the room while he waited for a response to his request. Serena walked along behind him as if expecting him to fall. Felicity folded her hands and clung to her hopes because screaming "What's going on?" wouldn't help. It might even hurt if the shock knocked Justin off-line.

"Terry, it's me," Justin said at last. "You were right, I was wrong, and I hope to hell I'm not too late—you did? He is? Oh. Good."

Then he stepped back and sat down. There was no chair behind him. Serena's timely grab kept him from landing on the floor. She got a seat into place, then retreated to her own chair at the table and began placidly demolishing a cupcake.

Felicity held her breath to keep hope and fear and all the questions inside, and she sat on her hands to keep from tearing the tablecloth. Her body felt as heavy as stone from the tension that she could not channel into her fingers.

Justin said, "Safety first, yes. Thanks." He crossed his arms on the table and rested his forehead on them. "Terry has him."

The snarled mess of emotions inside Felicity's chest threatened to burst out through her ribs. "Who," she asked, "is Terry? And what kind of phone works when the network is down?"

"Any phone within range of the workshop booster. Yours doesn't? There must be a syncing problem...never mind." Justin turned his head to peer at her. "Terry is the head of the security firm that guards this place."

"Guards?" Felicity latched onto the words that made sense. "Security?"

"Yes, security." Justin buried his face against his arms again. "I own fifty square klicks of land here, and there's a zillion-dollar R&D facility on it as well as my legal residence. I keep a low profile, but paparazzi still camp on the access roads. How did you think it was protected?"

Felicity hadn't thought about it at all. "Magic?"

That raised a muffled laugh from him. "Surveillance, patrols, inspections, travel protection, background checks. All very discreet."

"They are sneaky," Serena said. She slid a cupcake to Justin. "I'm sneakier. I spotted the team that shadows our field trips ages ago. Naomi will be cranky when she finds out."

"Please don't tell her," Justin said. "No one likes being watched all the time. Why do you think I keep quiet about it? Anyway, Terry's people are trained and equipped for worse weather than this, but they can't move fast in it. It might be midnight or later before they get Carl home."

Relief loosened Felicity's muscles enough that she could move again. *He's alive. He's safe.* The anger tightened its grip.

"I'll wait up," she said.

CHAPTER 13
WEE HOURS, DECEMBER 6

CARL PULLED THE KITCHEN door closed, and a heavy silence replaced the scratchy howl of snow-laden wind. The room was pitch dark and frigid cold.

Terry opened the door to the basement. Light painted the lower steps, and pine-scented hot air rolled out of the stairwell. A murmur of voices rose over the sound of flowing water.

"You got it from here, Doc?" Terry put a hand on Carl's arm. "Orders are to see you safe to the boss, but I hate to shuck layers while Kaylie and Keene are waiting outside."

Her touch delivered another message. Carl had been ignoring similar ones from the rest of the squad since he started thawing. *Pull yourself together,* was the silent admonishment. *Other people have worse problems. Why can't you cheer up? Why can't you see how good your life is?*

They had been nothing but kind, but the unspoken pressure was suffocating him. "I'd say you've gone above and beyond already," he said. "Your orders were to let me die in a snowdrift, weren't they?"

He kicked off his boots and unsealed his coat before starting a careful descent. His ribs ached every time he inhaled, and he was stiff as well as cold.

"Hang on a sec, Doc." Shame resonated in Terry's whisper. The snow goggles had left red marks on her brown, smooth skin, and water droplets beaded in her short black hair. She was solid muscle from neck to boots, and she radiated self-assurance, as always.

"I fought that order," she said. "We argued. He won."

"Justin usually does. He had his reasons." Leaving Carl that option, giving him the right to decide his own fate—it was a priceless gift to someone who been stripped of all choices more than once. "I understand why he did it."

"I don't," Terry said. "And Kaylie is furious with you. I'm sure you know that. We all keep wanting to kick you until you stop moping. I know it's wrongheaded, but we can't help it any more than you can snap out of the deep blue funk."

The comment was loaded with frustration, and for some reason it lifted Carl's spirits immensely. "Life isn't easy," he said. "Can I have a damned hug?"

Terry laughed and stomped down the steps to embrace him with brisk affection. "No more adventures tonight, please."

He resumed his downward progress, leaning heavily on the banister. As he reached the bottom, the voices resolved into an argument about bidding and card suits. Identical archways on either side led into short halls that blocked his view of the rooms.

He called out, "Pool room or rec room?"

"Pool room of course." Justin's raised voice came from the door to the right. "Why would I be in the drafty gym and sport zone when I have hot water, heated floors, and the same natural insulation in here?" Water splashed. "I cannot grasp why anyone would pick freezing over drowning."

The comment caught Carl off guard. He hadn't quite decided how to respond before he came around the corner, where Felicity met him with a hug so fierce it took his breath away. She wore thermal leggings and a tunic sweater that clung to her curves, and she had on winter boots that gave her an extra bump in height.

Carl wrapped both arms around her and leaned back, bringing her onto her tiptoes. Her hair tickled his nose. She was warm, soft and everything good in the world, she was real and solid in his arms...and she was trembling.

Carl's throat went tight around all the things he'd spent hours rehearsing in his head. He held on with all his strength and rocked her back and forth. Felicity pressed her face against his neck and sighed heavily.

The first thought that came into Carl's head popped out of his mouth. "Now I see why you find that habit so annoying."

Felicity's hands slid down his arms as she backed away. She laced her fingers with his. "I'm not apologizing. I am so upset I don't even know where to start."

Relief bubbled through her blustering words. There was plenty of real unhappiness, though, and all that seething emotion was hard to face. Carl looked over the room while he gathered his courage.

The basement of the house contained Justin's one extravagant personal indulgence. The space beneath and around the original foundation had been excavated and reinforced, and he'd transformed the resulting space into a roomy private refuge.

The concrete walls were molded and painted to the texture of rocky outcroppings, and murals offered vivid glimpses of evergreen forest beyond the rocks. Live plantings of conifers and ferns created protective bowers around seating groups, and a tile mosaic in greens and browns evoked the look of a leaf-strewn lawn underfoot.

Usually the ceiling displayed a sky accurate for the time and latitude, but tonight the lights behind the screen projected hazy blue noon-time brilliance. The warm air smelled damp and metallic.

The centerpiece of the grotto was a meandering stone-lined stream long and wide enough to serve as a lap pool. A cascading waterfall at one end disguised the outlet from its filtration system.

Justin stood next to the steaming whirlpool on the far side. Where Felicity's anger was fiery, he was icy: body tensed, shoulders low, eyes flat and cold, arms folded tight.

A low table next to him held cups, cards, and a datapad in a waterproof cover. Serena was sitting on the edge of the hot tub. She wore a candy-cane outfit and a sad frown, and she was leaning forward with one hand clasped around Justin's wrist.

"Lucky bird," she said. "Crashing where kind hands could lift you up to the nest again. Lucky to be alive."

She is perceptive in that skewed way of hers. Carl turned to Felicity.

He should promise that it would never come that close again. He should swear he'd turned a corner and seen the light and all the other recovery clichés in the world, because Felicity deserved surety. The lies were all right there on the tip of his tongue. *Don't,* he told himself desperately. *Don't do it.*

He said, "It seems we're at an impasse."

Felicity waited. Carl raised an eyebrow at her. "I won't make excuses or apologize for being sick. You won't apologize for being worried sick. A fight is imminent."

The corners of Felicity's mouth drew up. "Stop it. Don't look at me like that. I'm trying to stay upset at you."

Justin said, "And I'm getting cold, waiting for you to bring him close enough for me to kick his ass. Get a room or get over here."

Carl left the choice to Felicity by raising an enquiring eyebrow. She rolled her eyes. "Don't push your luck, country boy. Come in and sit down. We have negotiating to do."

Negotiating. He contemplated all the possibilities inherent in that word. It had a hopeful ring to it.

FELICITY COULD NOT BEGIN to hold back all the feelings that made her hands shake and her eyes sting. Concentrating on practicalities kept her from collapsing in a breathless heap of doubt. *What will I do if he says no?* That was the question she kept asking herself. Her unhappy answer was: *Keep helping him fight until he loses and breaks my heart in the process.*

She took Carl to the largest of the room's seating groups: three couches and a table set well away from the pool where Justin was bundling back into his clothes. That confrontation could wait a little while longer.

Serena was talking to thin air. Felicity hoped it was another conversation with Naomi and not an argument with herself. Naomi had been calling every half hour since Justin sent some kind of data package to her phone along with an apology. Felicity still felt an unseemly amount of satisfaction that Naomi hadn't been given a magic phone either.

The couches inside the miniature grove looked as if they'd grown there. Carl dropped into the middle of the center one, slid down the leaf-patterned upholstery until his head was propped on a cushion, and stretched out his legs.

Then he sighed.

"Jerk," Felicity said.

He smiled and edged to one side, opening up seat space. Felicity was reminded of the way the tabby cat had flirted with her, especially when Carl patted the cushion. The smile was all he had going for him. His face was wind-chapped and scruffy, and his cheeks looked sunken below bruised-looking eyes. Deep lines of fatigue bracketed his lips and nose.

He had on a heavy white coat and snow pants, he was slumped inelegantly in the seat, and Felicity wanted to curl up with him and listen to his heartbeat for a few million hours.

No. Tempting, but no. "I'm not sitting there," she said. "You're distracting, and we need to talk."

His eyelids drooped shut. "Your loss."

I nearly lost you forever, you jackass. "I'll make up for it later if you'll stop teasing. Otherwise I'm calling your bluff on the PDA, and with Serena involved, I promise you'll regret it."

His eyes popped open, and he sat up straight. "I'm all ears."

Justin limped into the bower. "What a bizarre image," he said. "That would be a lot of ears."

Carl replied, "Do you know the one about killing someone with kindness?"

The silence went thick. Finally Justin said, "I'm glad Terry took the initiative, but I would still stand by my order even if she'd let you turn into an icicle. I will not cage you. Hate me if you want."

He pulled a twig off one of the plants and stripped needles from it one at a time. Carl watched the falling debris with a stony expression. Felicity went to retrieve her project bag and her drink before the emotional pressure crushed her.

Serena had finished talking and was picking up cards. "That was Naomi," she said, confirming Felicity's earlier guess. "She's such a big bundle of worry that she won't believe good even when she feels it."

And it's my fault that she's stuck in Lincoln. "I'm sorry," Felicity said.

Serena shook her head. "No, that isn't right. I was meaning 'thank you,' so you say 'you're welcome.' Distance is better when Bao can't find a steady spot in the middle of us. I wish I could move her like you do, but my claws are too flashy. You're all soft and sneaky-silent, and she never sees you until you've grabbed her up and dropped her down into a happy spot. I want to learn that. More hot chocolate, first. Carl is all frosty."

She marched up the stairs.

Justin sleeps with that, and he thinks "all ears" is bizarre? Felicity gathered her yarn and beads and took a seat on the couch across from Carl. "Enough," she said. "Hug, punch, or talk, but get it over with."

Carl sighed and got to his feet, but that silent pressure only got worse and worse. Felicity held her breath. *Please don't fight.*

Both of them went for the hug at the last second. Felicity cleared her throat to keep from giggling with relief. Justin looked like a baby penguin, all dressed in charcoal gray, surrounded by Carl's sleeves and tucked in under the taller man's chin.

"Fluffy birds," Serena said when she arrived with a carafe and a steaming mug. The cup was thrust at Carl. "*Cold* bird. Justin, be a blanket for him. You're always warm."

Both men sat down, although Justin ignored the blanket suggestion. Serena plucked the branch away from him. "And stop hurting the bushes. They live in little boxes of dirt for you. You should be grateful."

Justin's initially blank reaction to the scold made Felicity wonder if they'd lost him. Then he smiled that bright, unaffected grin of his. "I am grateful," he said. "For you, above all things. Settle, crazy woman."

Serena flopped down on Carl's other side with a happy noise just short of a purr. He shifted his weight to protect his drink from being jostled, and he raised that eloquent eyebrow at Felicity. "This is a negotiation?"

"It's a start." Stringing a few beads gave Felicity a chance to collect her thoughts. "We spent our evening discussing ways to minimize the risk of repeating an evening like this, and I've noticed that you listen better when people sit on you."

Color rose in Carl's cheeks. There were some very specific, very *personal* memories associated with that observation. "I'm listening," he said.

Serena squirmed around until she could put her legs over Carl's lap. "What you need to do is to fly. Birds *fly*."

"You had a career once," Justin said in translation. "One you chose. One you were good at, or so I'm told."

Carl gave him a long look. "I can't go back into therapeutic work. It's been eight years. I'm no longer remotely proficient. Worse, I'm a predator now. Anyone vulnerable enough to need psychiatric help would look like prey, and I could not live with myself if I—"

He set down his mug and scrubbed both hands over his face. "I know I need direction. Recognizing a hole and filling it are two different things."

"Stop trying to be nothing," Serena said. "You need to be what you are now, like I am. You need to do what I've done."

Carl turned to her, frowning. Watching them in profile, Felicity finally realized why she found Serena's stares so disconcerting. She associated that intensity so strongly with Carl that it looked wrong on anyone else.

Carl said gently, "Your unique way of coping isn't for me."

"Of course not," Serena said. "I have a whole zoo in my head to help. Your den is cold and empty. You need to look outside, not in. You need a flock. A big one, not our little us-flock."

"Hawks don't fly in flocks." Carl picked up his cup and downed the cocoa in one gulp. "They also don't have dens."

"Don't be a shit," Justin said. "You know what she means. You wanted isolation, but you only got better once we stopped letting you isolate yourself."

"Meaningful work and human contact don't cure depression, but they can help," Felicity said. "And if you're going to keep jumping, you need a bigger safety net."

"Says the mental-health professional," Carl said.

Sarcastic sniping is a rearguard action. We are getting through. I hope. Felicity parried with facts. "The stress of elite artistic performance does not promote mental stability. Every last soul in my extended family goes in for regular depression screenings, and all of us learn and practice support strategies. Did you think I was born knowing how to be patient with your bullshit?"

Carl blinked.

Serena laughed out loud and bounced to her feet. "See? I see it! *That's* how you do it. Swoop. Pounce. Plop. Do you still need me here? I want to run so I can think on that."

"In the gym," Justin said. "With clothes on."

"Because snow and cameras, yes, yes." She waved a dismissive hand and jogged away.

"What happens if I shred the safety net?" Carl said. "I cannot be trusted not to push people around, even when I don't mean to do it. You've seen that often enough. What kind of flock can you imagine inflicting me on?"

That's my cue. Felicity set down the bracelet and smiled at him. "Mine. I've been threatening to introduce you to my family for weeks now. Let's do it."

JUSTIN MADE it most of the way through discussing details before he faded out. After Serena collected him and led him unsteadily off to bed, Felicity took one look at Carl's befuddled face and chivvied him upstairs too.

Worry tugged at her nerves again once they were snuggling together under the quilts. Carl still shivered occasionally, and he was cold to the touch despite the flannel and sweats he'd worn to bed.

"You are out of danger, aren't you?" she asked. "A doctor checked you out, right? Hypothermia is serious business."

Carl's answer was to put his arm over his face, which was not encouraging. The longer the silence went on, the more tempting retaliation got. Felicity sat up and ran her fingers through his hair.

"Cornrows, I think," she said. "It'll take forever, as fine as this is, but I'm up for it."

"Don't you dare," Carl muttered.

"Or what? You'll kill yourself?" Felicity bit down on her tongue. She wanted so badly to let it go, but anger kept popping up in bitter bubbles whenever she relaxed. "That was cruel. I'm sorry."

Carl lowered his arm, capturing Felicity's hand in the process, and rolled onto his side. "Or I will shave my head bald," he said.

His palm was cool against Felicity's wrist, but he was smiling in that slow-burn way of his that made her insides melt. Her laughter rode a swelling tide of relief. "You would look ridiculous."

"Nothing could look more ridiculous than blond cornrows." Carl lay back again, pressing Felicity's hand to his chest as if he knew how much she needed to feel his heartbeat strong and slow under her fingertips.

He probably does. Arrogant mind-reading magic at work. There were no objections when Felicity laid her head on his ribs. She slipped her hand under his shirt too, skin against rough-textured skin.

His voice rumbled against her ear when he finally spoke. "Am I out of danger? Physically, yes. Keene—she's the security company's doctor—injected a med monitor because she didn't like my cardio rhythm, but I'm warming up. It's a slow process, that's all."

"Physically out of danger." Felicity couldn't overlook that careful clarification. Not after tonight. "You are not reassuring me, Carl."

His pulse thumped a little faster, and his chest felt like rock under Felicity's hand: cool, hard, and unmoving.

"What's wrong?"

"Life is a slow process too," he said. "I can't give you certainty. I can't give you any guarantees."

Felicity listened to the steady thump of moving blood beneath her ear, and her own heart sped up. *Now or never* wasn't quite the right description for what she felt, but there was no point in waiting.

"Let me give you something, then. My answer is yes." Her heart sank when Carl didn't respond. *Maybe he didn't understand. He is tired.* "Yes, I will step into your brother's shoes. I will be your anchor or your center or whatever you call it. I said would give you my answer when I decided, and I have. Yes."

Carl rolled over, and Felicity ended up spooned against him, held in place by his arms. "*Not* replacing my brother," he murmured in her ear. "That is a whole file of mental images I do not need. Is calling you my salvation too melodramatic?"

"Worse." *Even if it is gratifying.* "Trite."

He dropped a kiss on the nape of Felicity's neck, sending shivers all the way to her toes. "Can I say I love you now?" he asked.

Felicity let herself lie quiet and relaxed in the cradle of his arms and waited. The panic didn't come. "Yes, I think you can."

"Excellent." His lips moved to the point of her shoulder. "Your plan to meet your family scares the hell out of me. I deserve some small compensation."

"It scares *you*?" Felicity gasped as cold hands went exploring under her night shirt. "You don't know enough about them to be properly frightened."

"How so?"

Family was the last thing Felicity wanted to discuss. "Do you really want to hear about my childhood traumas now? I had other ideas."

When Carl started laughing, it was the gentle, joyful rumble that always seemed to surprise him as much as it thrilled Felicity. "You are full of ideas tonight," he said.

It sounded like a tease, but his hands were no longer moving, and he made no move to pick up the pace. And then he shivered again.

"Carl..."

"I'm fine," he said. "That med-monitor will be broadcasting for a day or more, and it's tied into the security net. If my vitals drop, Keene will be on the phone yelling about it in three seconds flat."

Light dawned for Felicity. The monitor would also be broadcasting when Carl's vitals rose, so to speak. *Someone's feeling shy.* She turned in Carl's arms and pressed close, grinning into his blue eyes from a hand's-breadth away. *But not too shy.* "Too late for stage fright. I can tell the curtain's already up."

He smiled back and kissed her. "Showtime," he murmured.

THE FARM DIDN'T LOOK its best in winter. The mountains were lost to sight, wrapped in dull, misty clouds, and the forest surrounding the pastures became a gloomy wall of bare black tree limbs and drooping wet evergreen boughs.

It was a dismal sight, but in Felicity's opinion, the warmth made up for the dreary view. The sky might be murky and the ground soggy, but the damp air that kissed her cheeks felt positively balmy after the last few weeks of frigid Nebraska winds.

At the top of the parking lot trail, the lawn spread out on both sides with the bright-lit cozy lodge at center stage. No tents huddled in the pastures for this revel. The weather was too unpredictable, and the attendance was low enough to house everyone in the lodge's guest rooms and the twelve rustic cabins behind it.

The creaking porch rockers held elders enjoying the fresh air and dogs who had been evicted from furniture indoors. Felicity's shouted greeting was met with a few desultory waves and a bark or two.

She inhaled the heady scent of home, with its unique blend of greenery, drifting smoke and wet farm animals, and she gave Carl a smile. "What do you think?"

Carl lifted each boot and lowered it in place, squishing mud into their clean treads. His bright blue winter coat was so new it still had creases, and it made a beautiful contrast with his hair, like sunshine and clear sky. He scowled at the lodge while he swung his weekend bag idly in one hand as if preparing to throw it at someone. Felicity cleared her throat. "Carl?"

He took a deep breath. "I'm too scared to think, and I hurt people when I feel vulnerable."

"Not with me around, you won't. I'll slap you back fast if you cross the line from jerk to manipulator." *Wasn't that the whole point of all the work we did, the last few weeks?* "My brain is full of keywords and warning signs, remember?"

"There's a fairly long stretch of spectrum between civilized behavior and slipping far enough into sociopathy to warrant a neurological ass-kicking."

"Pulling out all the vocabulary stops *and* using expletives?" Felicity took his hand and gave his wrist a quick kiss. "You are fretting, aren't you? Listen. Unless you get radically worked up, no one will notice. Have you paid any attention to my stories? This crowd thinks of barbed commentary and verbal beatings as casual conversation. Berating others is an art form."

Carl exhaled on a chuckle. "This is a selling point?"

"Yes," Felicity said. "You are about to be surrounded by people who think it's fun to out-emote each other. If you bite someone's head off, you'll get applause. I think you'll fit in. If I'm wrong and you can't take it, you'll tell me, and we'll go."

A hurried departure would surprise no one. Dramatic exits

were as much a staple of revels as heated debates and social one-upmanship.

"What about them?" Carl looked over his shoulder at the trio still trudging slowly uphill through the woods.

Naomi was in the lead, with Justin with Serena right behind. Their winter gear matched Carl's, differing only in the bright colors; the three dark heads bobbing along in height order made them look like a set of coordinated nesting dolls in red, green, and yellow, respectively. Justin was laughing at some remark Serena had just made, and Naomi was as wide-eyed and alert as a cat with a new feather toy.

"Stop worrying. They will have fun with or without us."

"Parties are always fun until Justin goes off-line and someone pulls out a camera. There's a reason he's a recluse, Felicity."

Carl headed across the muddy grass toward the lodge. Felicity hurried after him, thinking, *Now you're borrowing trouble.* Justin hadn't slipped into one of his dazes for a week now. "I understand why he hates public appearances, but I've told you, this place is a sanctuary. Minimal electronics, no phones, no cameras, no gawking."

Security wouldn't be a problem, not with four of Terry's armed Amazons swapping war stories with the Gearys and getting oriented at the gatehouse. There was a time-honored solution to the issue of Justin's celebrity, too.

Carl said, "It can't be as simple as you say it will be."

"Yes, it can. Incognito is a respected stage tradition. He's Justin Romero on the guest list, and no matter how many people recognize him, that's all he'll be to them. Stop looking for reasons to be anxious."

Justin would be treated kindly if he treated others well, and that seemed to come naturally to him. Even at his oddest he was less disruptive than any of the old uncles and aunts who got intoxicated and told bloody Restoration stories. He was the least of Felicity's worries.

Carl stopped in his tracks. "I'm not the only one anxious. You're wound up too. You're hiding it, but it's there. Why?"

"I'm worried about my mother." Felicity pulled her courage out from underneath her frayed nerves and forced herself to smile. "We aren't speaking. I've never brought anyone to a revel because it's harder to avoid her with a guest on hand. I intend to try. Let's make a deal. If you need to run away, you'll tell me, and if I need to run, I'll tell you. Fair?"

"Deal." Carl flicked a watchful eye at their approaching friends, then raised his eyebrows at her. His eyes were twinkling. "I feel better already."

CHAPTER 15
AFTERNOON, DECEMBER 19

THE WOMAN WHO APPROACHED them as soon as they entered the lodge looked harmless enough to Carl on first glance. Her hair was gray, but age had been kind to her lean body, and she had a lively smile on her wrinkled face. Then he noticed it was Felicity's smile, framed by features that could have been stamped from the same mold.

All similarity ended at the eyes. The mother's gaze was a familiar shade of brown, but it held all the warmth of polished stone. Carl didn't need to look at Felicity to sense her confidence crumbling. The tension was like a silent mutter of apprehension. He put a hand on her waist: *You can do this.*

Her knuckles tightened on the strap of her bag. "Nice ambush, Mother."

"Oh, Flee, how could I resist?" The woman held out both hands in supplication. "When Papa Joe said you were bringing guests for Solstice, I thought, what a perfect opportunity to reconcile. I'm so glad you're here."

She wore a fluttery layered caftan, and the delicate material emphasized a lithe grace that spoke of dance training. Her light-footed elegance made Felicity's stolid defensive posture look clumsy in contrast.

Carl flinched as insight hit hard. The woman deliberately dressed and moved that way. She *wanted* Felicity to feel awkward. A surge of protective fury blindsided him before he caught himself short, and Felicity elbowed him in warning. This was her fight. If she wanted help, she would ask.

Her mother said, "Please don't sulk, Flee. I've been waiting forever for this chance. Give me a hug and introduce me to your handsome beau."

Felicity ignored the outstretched hands. "Mother, this is Carl Jenson. Carl, meet Victoria Chen. My mother. Better known to the world as the chairman for the Chen division of Oregon Arts and Entertainments."

"The nation's leading live performance company," Victoria said, beaming as she added the accolade. She gave Carl a visual once-over that left him feeling self-conscious, then offered a handclasp that lingered. "I'm thrilled to meet you. Has Felicity warned you that she swore off marriage and family to spite me?"

"I did not say that. I said that you would never see a child from me." Felicity paused. "*After* you told me there was no room at your hearth for a merchant's apprentice unless I wanted to breed my way into your good graces."

"Was it so wrong to want more grandchildren?" Victoria turned slightly as she spoke. Carl gritted his teeth on a sneer about playing to the audience.

The lodge was a wood-beamed rustic relic from an era when old-growth trees were an acceptable construction material, and it had been built to the scale of the surrounding mountains. People traveled up and down a wide set of stairs in groups, and others were lined up near at a pair of tables in rows. Voices rose to ceiling of the main room, which was open to the rafters three floors up.

"Why are you still dwelling on this after all these years?" Victoria turned back to confront Felicity. "You jumped to conclusions from an offhand remark. I know Joy's told you that more than once. Why do you cling to this silly grudge? Can't you meet me halfway, dearest?"

She held out her hands again. A hush fell over the room as their audience awaited the next move. Threat of public disapproval was a powerful motivator for some people. Others dug in their heels harder. Victoria didn't understand her daughter at all.

Felicity said, "We have nothing to say to each other, Mother."

Victoria let her arms fall to her sides and made the critical error of appealing to Carl. "I do hope you'll try to convince her. You can see I only want what's best, can't you?"

Oh, yes, I see. Victoria believed she was hard on her loved ones for their own good, a martyr to the cause of perfection, her sacrifices never appreciated or understood. That self-image was rooted in a well-exercised sense of entitlement and an unshakable belief that kindness was weakness.

She was a selfish, petty tyrant whose only definition of best was based on self-interest. Carl forced his hands to unclench, but the urge to take her down would not be suppressed.

Felicity's hand slid into his. Her fingers were cold, and she offered him a wan smile. Carl put his other hand over hers. "Let me fix this?"

Her eyes widened at the coded request. Her pulse jumped against his fingers, but she nodded, whispering, "Go for it. You're cleared for action."

Carl felt chains fall away inside his mind. He caught Victoria's eye and put on his *best* smile. Opportunities to cut loose the full force of his personality without guilt were rare. He took full advantage. Charm was a matter of controlling uncountable tiny physical cues. He could let charisma ooze from every pore when it suited him.

It suited him to hammer Victoria down fast and hard.

"Have you ever apologized?" he asked. "In person, I mean. It sounds like the real issue is that you're both too stubborn to say you're sorry."

He pitched his voice with precision, so that the words carried to the spectators on the stairs without sounding forced. Capturing their undivided attention was worth the pain from Felicity's nails biting into his wrist.

Victoria's lips thinned. Carl followed up the solid hit to the woman's temper with a more subtle cut. "If you want to meet halfway then you should go first, don't you think? Demonstrate that you're the mature, reasonable one."

He waited, eyes locked on Victoria's. It was a simple ego trap. She was too self-righteous to see an apology as anything other than submission and surrender, but appearances meant everything. Refusal would look like spite.

Her sidelong glance at the spectators was all Carl needed to see. He stepped close, as if to plead in privacy, and let his manner harden into pure menace. "Keep your distance until hell freezes over, and you get to keep your moral high ground here and now. Confront us again, and I will make you regret it. Try anything behind our backs, and I will destroy you. Do I make myself clear?"

Victoria's nod was a bare jerk of her chin. Carl broke the spell with a shrug and a softening of body language, relaxing back to public charm as he smiled at Felicity. *Please catch this hint.* "I'm glad one of you can be reasonable. What about you, Flee? Are you ready to apologize?"

"Not a chance." She said it with every appearance of outrage, but the spark in her eyes was amusement.

"Well, I tried." He pulled Felicity forward by the hand, right past her mother. "Let's go, Flee."

Felicity kept up her act of disgruntled disappointment throughout the check-in process, even when the others caught up and Naomi sent Carl a puzzled look. *Later,* Carl told her silently with a shake of his head.

Once they reached their assigned cabin behind the lodge, Felicity wrapped her arms around him and released the laughter she'd been holding inside. He buried his face in her hair and drove back seeping doubts with that happy approval.

He had lost his temper, but he hadn't annihilated Victoria publicly and permanently. He'd hadn't lost control. Felicity's faith in him might be justified after all.

"Magnificent," she said when she caught her breath.

She's happy. Be satisfied. Carl inspected the spartan accommodations: two single beds, one to a side, with a small bathroom and a counter at the back. "We have different definitions of magnificent."

"Jerk. You know what I meant." She planted a kiss on his lips. "This could be worse. The other side has bunk beds. We share the bathroom, too. You'll want to lock both sides if you don't want Serena barging in."

"Noted." The doors would stay unlocked. He would rather be interrupted than shut in.

Felicity ducked into the bathroom. "I call dibs on washing up first."

The beds were more comfortable than they looked, if a bit

short. Carl stretched out and closed his eyes. It had been a long trip, and alternating long immobile intervals with exertion was a recipe for sore joints. The sounds of running water and Felicity's humming voice were soothing, as were the assorted various thumps and murmurs from the adjoining room. Exhaustion took over.

HE WOKE to the sound of hushed giggles.

"He'll have five job offers before the night's over, wait and see." That was Felicity. "I'd never ever seen him turn *on*, like that. Talk about stage presence!"

Serena's voice approached. "He flies along, all dazzling, and then swoop, grab, snap, he's got someone by the throat." Something poked Carl's shoulder. "I know you're awake again, silly bird. Pull your head out from under your wing. It's time for supper."

He sat up, feeling barely a twinge from his chest muscles for once. Serena retreated to join the other two, who sat cross-legged on the other bed. Naomi was holding a skein of yarn across her hands while Felicity wound it into a ball.

Felicity's soft sweater and pants were earth-toned and textured, which suited her, while Serena and Naomi preferred bright sleek tops and leggings that brought out the blue highlights in their hair. They looked comfortable and *right* together, complementary strengths shining past the surface contrasts.

Naomi's face was crinkled up into a smile so wide her eyes got lost in it, and Serena was biting her upper lip. Carl looked to Felicity for an explanation.

"You snore," she informed him.

"Cute little burbles," Naomi rushed to assure him. Serena nodded. "Like a kitten. Let's go to the lodge. I need to feed Justin."

"He isn't here?"

Naomi said, "No, still in the lodge. Some ancient man overheard him gushing about the solar panels during check-in. Then came the handshakes and the back slapping, and the technical questions started, and they wandered off together."

Felicity said, "Papa Joe may keep him up all night. Updating the property was his idea, and he's proud of the results."

Her tone implied that others hadn't been as pleased.

There was more. Carl waited for the rest of it. Felicity grinned. "Papa Joe is also as close as we get to ultimate authority around here. Justin couldn't ask for a better guardian angel. Come to supper and say hello to him yourself."

The meal proved to be a casual affair, and one that Carl enjoyed immensely to his own surprise. After choosing selections from an extensive buffet, they tracked down Justin and Papa Joe in a corner seating area. A datapad, a phone and a sketch board were all in use. The two of them were so deeply involved in their discussion that if Serena hadn't brought them plates and cups, they both probably would've missed the meal altogether.

Carl idly wondered what they were planning when he wasn't enjoying the rest of the entertainment. Justin had a gift for finding useful allies. From the occasional mention of Ryan's name, future visitations were being planned.

This trip is opening up new horizons for everyone. A working farm full of history would be a much better environment for a little boy than Justin's retreat. Carl smiled, picturing Ryan's reaction to the goats, and then realized he was thinking about the future without dread for the first time in recent memory.

Most of the people attending the increasingly rowdy party ate standing up or clustered around tables that were set up or folded away as needed. Early on, Felicity pointed out her immediate family's territorial claim—a table surrounded by tall, busty women, big, muscular men and children ranging from infancy to adolescence—but she named no one, and clearly had no intention of initiating contact.

Carl had anticipated a boisterous and flamboyant crowd, but the crush and noise exceeded his wildest expectations. If anything, Felicity's descriptions of her relatives had been conservative. Sarcasm, hyperbole, and rhetorical flourishes were happily cast out like clouds of verbal glitter, punctuated by rapid-fire exchanges of quoted dialogue and random outbursts of song.

It would've taken a determined effort on his part to make more than a momentary ripple in the roaring social flow. He felt no need to exert himself. Experiencing it was satisfying enough without interacting.

A stage combat demonstration began on the open second-floor balcony, and Serena was recruited as a prop master. Then Naomi was swept away by a rambunctious huddle of youngsters who were setting up a dessert buffet. She looked as happy as Carl could ever remember seeing her, surrounded by a sea of bouncing heads and waving little hands.

Last, Felicity was whirled off into an impromptu dance by a pair of cousins whose gingery hair and willowy bodies made Carl marvel at the mysteries of genetics and the flexibility inherent in the concept of family. No one challenged his solitude, but it never felt like exclusion. Respect and acceptance were the messages carried on frequent glances and inviting smiles, and the few who attempted conversation moved on without offense when nothing developed.

Watching the ebb and flow was hypnotic. He woke from a half-doze when Naomi stopped in front of him. She had both hands covering her mouth, and her eyes were brimming with tears. Carl came to his feet in a rush of alarm. "What's wrong? What happened?" *What did I do now?*

It was a reasonable reaction, given that he'd been the cause of so much distress for so long, but when Naomi dropped her hands the gesture revealed a joyful smile. Tears spilled down her cheeks. "You're better. I was afraid it was only me hoping. It wasn't. You're healing."

"No. There's no healing this. I'm balancing better for now. That's as good as it will get." He held out his hands. "Forgive me for shoving you so hard when I was staggering."

"Oh, you. There's nothing to forgive, except that you talk too much." Naomi took his hands, then stepped into a hug without an instant's hesitation. Carl tightened his arms around her and savored the precious gesture of trust.

"Parker called," Naomi mumbled against his chest. "He'll be home next week. He's coming back to us." Then her fist thumped into Carl's back. "That's from him. Well, he said punch you in the nose for tricking him, but I won't do that."

Finally caught on, did he? Carl backed out of range. "I had to drive him away, Naomi. He isn't as strong as you are. Not that way. He doesn't know how to let me fight for myself."

"I know." Naomi sat down cross-legged on the couch and scowled at Carl like a grumpy pixie. "He's peeved at you."

Carl knew peeved didn't begin to cover how Parker felt. Distance had attenuated the tie between them, and Carl had tried to let the link wither from disuse, but it never broke. Parker's fury was seething magma.

"I have some big bridges to repair." *If they can be fixed at all.* Sadness welled up. He'd done the right thing for good reasons, but intentions only went so far.

"I'll help." Naomi's reply was prompt. "But Flee will help most if you let her. Why are you lurking back here instead of dancing with her? Get out there and fly, Serena would say."

Carl looked across the room. Felicity was one of a mob dancing arm-in-arm in a circle, feet flying in a complicated pattern that went faster with every repetition of the music until they all stumbled and crashed in a heap.

Laughter rose to the rafters.

"She invited you in," Naomi said. "Don't make her beg."

Felicity glanced back at their corner as she stood up. Wistful resignation in her eyes turned to delight when her gaze met Carl's.

He smiled for her, and he went to join the dance.

CHAPTER 16
WEE HOURS, DECEMBER 22

A FAINT SCRATCHING NOISE WOKE FELICITY from uneasy dreams. The night light from the bathroom cast a dim glow across the center of the floor. The quiet felt ominous, as if her fears had followed her from sleep to consciousness.

She slipped into clothes and checked the opposite bed. Carl was a large, unmoving shadow under the covers he'd pulled over his head. They'd been up since the solstice celebration at dawn, and the party had gone on all day.

He was breathing. Alive.

Carl slept like a rock when he did sleep, but Felicity restrained herself to smoothing the blankets over his shoulder. Her hands were cold enough to wake the dead. *Don't be greedy,* she told herself. *Don't wake him because you had a bad dream.*

Someone tapped at the cabin door, making her jump. The noise part of the dream had been real.

Bee Geary waited on the step outside. The glow-beads Felicity had braided into her hair that afternoon glimmered in the moonlight, but the security uniform and her skin were too dark to make out any other details. Rain pattered down in hard cold droplets.

Bee whispered, "Papa J's no-tech rule is a huge pain in my ass. Two conversations and a walk in the wet, all to get you down to the gatehouse. Why can't we call the cabins direct, I ask you?"

Felicity grabbed jacket and shoes and closed the door behind her. "You're on lodge relay tonight? Why do I have to go to the gatehouse? What's wrong?"

"Nothing's *wrong*." Bee made a floppy gesture. "Although I have no idea where we'll put a guest at this hour. Cee needs you to sign him in."

"A visitor? At this hour?" *Asking for me?* "Who?"

Bee consulted her wrist-screen. "Eddie Parker? He showed up with an invite code, but—hey, take a light, Flee."

Felicity paused long enough to accept the headlamp before hurrying off.

An interesting scene greeted her inside the gatehouse. Cee usually looked the consummate professional in his workaday uniform, but tonight a sappy smile was plastered across his broad features. He was leaning over the duty counter on his elbows, watching two small buff-colored puppies wrestle on the floor.

Cee's cousin Tee was on the desk tonight, and he was holding a fluffy white puppy at arm's length while he tickled its belly. He was as scrawny as his cousin was brawny, and his laugh sounded too large to come from such a narrow chest.

Parker knelt in the middle of the room with his back to the door. His skin was tanned dark, except for an edge around hair trimmed so short its color could not be discerned. The tips of his ears looked sunburned. He had one arm over the back of a large tricolored dog, and they both watched the pups with doting pride.

The dog's shaggy coat was shiny, and her ears were pricked and alert. She lifted her muzzle to scent the air. Parker came to his feet and spun around. His hands swept past belt and thigh before tightening into fists.

The knife and pistol he'd been seeking were on the check-in counter, safe in Cee's custody. Felicity's heart pounded against her ribs. *Be fair. You startled him first.* She caught Parker's hazel eyes and raised her hands. "Hi, there. Remember me?"

Parker gave her a wry grin. "Unforgettable," he said in his pleasant baritone drawl.

Felicity crossed her arms at him to ward off the smile. She hadn't realized how much she'd missed the man's energy and humor until he was here. "Naomi said you'd be home next week. This is neither your home nor next week. Do you know what time it is?"

Cee and Tee promptly found something important to do in the back of the office. They took Parker's weapons with them, but they left the sign-in pad on the counter. That was a vote of confidence, in its way.

The dog pressed tight against Parker's leg, and puppies came tumbling from all over the room to huddle under their mother's belly. Parker knelt to pet them each in turn, combing his fingers through their fur.

"Late?" he said in answer to Felicity's earlier question.

His shoulders were hunched under creased khaki fatigues, and the jacket was dirty and covered in dog hair. *Talking is his least favorite activity in the world,* Felicity reminded herself. *Let it go.*

She said, "Did you come here straight from Australia? How did you get six dogs into the country without a quarantine hold?"

Parker's lips moved a few times before he spoke. "Justin's money and tons of paperwork. It took forever. I meant to surprise Naomi over supper."

You could've called. Felicity smothered the spark of aggravation. "Well, you're in luck. There's a spare bunk, so you can surprise her without rousing the whole farm."

Luck was probably named Justin or Papa Joe, now that Felicity thought about it. *A pox on all you secretive people and your complicated surprises.*

She signed Parker onto the official guest roster and helped him load puppies into a carrier. He didn't ask about Carl, and the avoidance quickly tied Felicity's stomach in nervous knots. Carl and knitting were really all she and Parker had in common. She handed over a puppy and gave him an opening. "Naomi thinks you're coming back because Carl's stabilized."

"She's wrong," Parker said. "I missed her. That's all."

He didn't miss Carl. He didn't miss the brother he'd nearly died to save more than once, the one whose life he held in his hands, the one whose emotions he could share when he chose. *Oh, Carl. What did you do to cut him this deeply?*

Felicity couldn't begin to guess, and she couldn't think of a way to ask. She started to worry about what would happen when they met again.

Parker clipped a leash on the mother dog's collar, lifted the carrier, and raised his chin. *Conversation over.* Felicity took the hint and let him go first.

"What's the dog's name?" she asked when the silence on the dark trail started to feel oppressive. "And what kind is she?"

The rain was a constant cold patter on her scalp, and the poor dog looked like a soggy rat. Parker waited until they were past the lit oasis of the lodge before he answered. "Mix. Shepherd, cattle dog, dingo for sure," he said. "The Customs vets went over her gene scan a dozen times. I call her Tich. The rest are Naomi's to name."

Felicity steered him to their cabin on the end of the first row. "Five puppies is an extravagant homecoming present. One is traditional, isn't it?"

Parker glanced back with a weary frown, squinting in the headlamp glare. "Split up the family and break their hearts? Who do you think I am? Carl's the asshole who hurts other people to make his own life easier."

Some breaks could never be mended. Felicity knew that better than most. Tears welled up out of nowhere. She hurriedly wiped them away and tried to laugh off the discomfort. "Ouch. I walked right into that, didn't I?"

Her voice gave her away. Parker stopped. "Oh, fuck. Fucking words."

The carrier landed with a splash and a chorus of yapping protests from its occupants. Parker pulled Felicity into a damp, squishy embrace that was ultimately comforting, even if it did smell like dog and sweat and stale coffee. Felicity gave him an extra squeeze when she had the weepiness under control. *Maybe nothing will be the same, but this is hopeful.*

"Thanks," she whispered, and she kissed Parker on his wet stubbly cheek to prove she meant it.

Carl's voice came out of the nearby darkness like a roll of thunder. "Is this revenge, brother? I threaten yours, you make a play for mine?"

The deep, brutal tone made Felicity's skin prickle with goose bumps. *That is dangerously close to pushing-voice.*

Parker turned without releasing her. Her lamp flashed across the cabin porch. Carl stood in the doorway with one hand braced high on the frame. He looked like a ghost, in black sweatpants that left his pale chest and face floating in shadow.

The meaning of his words sank into Felicity's heart like shards of ice. If that meant what she thought it did, then her role in this little melodrama was a lot more complicated than she'd realized.

"*That* was his ultimatum?" she asked Parker. "He told you he would seduce Naomi if you didn't hit the road?"

"Worse." His fingers dug into Felicity's arm. "Proved he could, first."

Carl said, "Get your hands off her, Eddie."

"It isn't what you thin—"

Naomi peeked through the gap between Carl's raised arm and his body. She looked even more ethereal than usual in a long white sleep shirt. "Parker?" Her voice was a drowsy purr. "What are you doing here?"

Someone next to Felicity growled. It wasn't the dog.

"Parker, no, they weren't—crap." Felicity grabbed him, but her efforts were as effective as grabbing an ocean wave. He charged straight into Carl. They hit the floor with a crash. Naomi yelped and leaped back.

Tich started barking. Felicity grabbed the dog's leash before she could bolt after her owner. Farm dogs answered with howls and baying, and other cabin windows lit up.

Carl and Parker came rolling out of the cabin and slid across the wet lawn, digging a wide, muddy furrow as they went. Someone in the lodge flipped on the yard floodlights. Felicity groaned. *Perfect. What's a farce without an audience?*

Naomi darted past flailing arms and legs, and water in the grass splashed over her bare feet. She frowned at the crate full of crying puppies, and her eyes widened at the gathering crowd of witnesses.

"What is going on?" she asked plaintively. "I heard voices. Why are they both so angry?"

Felicity bit her tongue. *Where do I start?* Her appreciation for absurdity was the only thing holding her temper and fears in check. "Based on underwhelming evidence, Carl has decided I'm screwing Parker, who apparently thinks you're screwing Carl because Carl threatened to make a move on you."

"Oh." Naomi's sigh of exasperation turned into an exasperated squeak. "*Oh.* I have gone over and over this with him. How many times do I have to swear there's nothing? He can *feel* there's nothing, and he's still jealous. Why did I have to fall in love with a caveman?"

"I am asking myself the same thing. Should we turn a hose on them or let them fight it out?"

Naomi's impish smile made a brief appearance. "Let them beat each other up. It'll save us the effort later."

That was fine in concept, but the audience was still growing. Felicity spotted her oldest brother in the crowd and pointed to the lodge. Clement ducked indoors. Drastic events called for drastic measures. This performance would keep people up all night gossiping unless Papa Joe invoked a curfew.

"Serena's awake." Naomi said out of nowhere. Her teeth chattered. "I suppose I should go calm her down before she jumps into this too."

"No, don't." Felicity shrugged out of her coat and offered it to Naomi along with Tich's leash. "You take these. If I can't talk sense to the nitwits, then a dose of Serena might be the next best thing."

The men were locked in some complicated wrestling hold.

Parker had lost his coat and most of his shirt. All the wet, mud-slicked muscles made an impressive display. Felicity wondered long they could hold out before one of them slipped.

Carl made a pained noise, and Parker grunted. Felicity took a deep breath. "That is enough. Stop it."

She used the tone that she normally reserved for children running in store aisles. It worked equally well on adults. They couldn't freeze in their tracks, being immobile already, but they did shift their attention from each other to her.

Their eyes blazed with animosity. *Great. I'm the new target.* Felicity matched their anger with her own outrage. "Are you both braindead? Do you even know the meaning of the words respect and trust? We are not toys for you to fight over. Don't make me pull out the big stick, Carl. Don't make me drop you."

Parker jerked slightly, hearing that, and Felicity said, "Yes, hothead, he added me to his takedown team. Me. Not Naomi." *Please don't make me prove it. I don't want him helpless. I don't trust you not to kill him with your bare hands, not in this mood.* "Not that it matters. You don't own Naomi. He can't steal what isn't yours."

Parker's face tightened, and Felicity realized her mistake. Unlike any normal man, Carl could've stolen Naomi's affections. He hadn't, but he could have. Instead, he'd done everything in his power to keep her at a distance even when he hurt her and himself in the process. *We definitely need to work on that martyr complex.*

Carl shook his head, and Parker took ruthless advantage of the hesitation to flip him over and grab him around the neck from behind. Carl broke the chokehold by heaving himself to his feet and tossing Parker forward over his own head. The squishy thump of impact made the ground vibrate underfoot. Parker bounced up without hesitation, and they were grappling again in an instant. *So much for a rational, peaceful solution.*

Serena came streaking past, laughing and whooping at the top of her lungs as she launched herself into the fray.

Is she naked? No. Tights and boots. Better than nothing.

Her arrival acted like a drop of soap hitting oily water. She landed on top of both men, and they rolled in opposite directions as fast as they could. Everyone ended up with a fresh, thick coating of mud.

The entrance earned Serena a smattering of applause from the crowd of onlookers. Parker got as far as his knees before Serena's next leaping charge sent him skidding backwards and knocked him flat again. Serena locked both legs around his throat and squeezed tight while she hit him on the head with one hand.

"No," she said with each openhanded smack. "No, no, *no.*"

The applause from the audience yielded to laughter when Parker limited his resistance to shielding his head with one arm and waving for mercy with the other hand. Carl staggered upright. Felicity intercepted him before he could interfere by planting one hand on his chest.

"That's enough melodrama for one night," she said. "Is anything broken?"

He had to answer with a shake of his head because he was breathing too hard to speak. Rain trickled down his face, cutting pale trails in the mud. He combed sticky hair out of the way so he could wipe his eyes clear.

Serena howled with laughter again, distracting Felicity. Parker was swinging her around in a tight embrace as if they were the world's muddiest pair of ballroom dancers. Naomi stepped forward, smiling. Parker stepped from one woman to the other as smoothly as if they'd practiced the handoff, and he wrapped both arms around Naomi's slight form with a tenderness that brought a lump into Felicity's throat.

Naomi squirmed loose and clouted him on the shoulder with a balled fist before standing on tiptoe to lock lips with him. *That's where the whole soul mate thing must come in handy.* No need for long explanations and reconciliations. Felicity looked into Carl's eyes, saw a twinkle in the blue depths, and wondered if he was thinking the same thing.

"Jerk," she said. "I am a human being, not a prize. You don't get to tell me how to live or who to love. Ever."

"I have it on good authority that Eddie and I are both hauling around some heavy cultural baggage," Carl said. "That was only the most recent of a long series of demonstrations. It won't be the last, I'm sure."

Felicity looked long and hard at him. *How can I stay angry when he puts his soul in his eyes like that?* "We could already be kissing if you'd started with an apology."

"And waste all those big words?" Carl put his dirty bare arms around her and gave her a gritty kiss. "I am sorry."

Good. "If I ever leave you, I'll do it with prior warning and without betrayal. I promise. Put that in your bag of hang-ups and hold on tight."

The yard lights flicked off and on again, and Papa Joe sent people hurrying off to their beds with a loud whistle and a comment about pots, kettles, and threats to start telling stories on the lodge speaker system.

Serena slammed the cabin's front door shut behind her.

Felicity's heart sank when Papa Joe pointed directly at her from the back porch of the lodge and then crooked his finger at all of them in a summons. *That looks like trouble.*

It wasn't.

The party ended up in Papa Joe's big apartment in the lodge. The food and drinks laid out in the sitting room near the lit fireplace confirmed Felicity's suspicions about prior planning. She was not about to complain, not when she knew how comfortable the double beds in his guest rooms would be.

She did wonder whether Papa Joe would go with the *"best-laid schemes"* quote, or *"All's well that ends well."*

"All's well that ends well," he said before he left them to their own devices. A few minutes later Justin arrived with a damp, clean, mostly dressed Serena at his back, and dry clean clothes for everyone in his arms. He greeted the room with the words, "Oh, well, best-laid plans and all," and Felicity had to explain why she was laughing so hard tears ran down her face.

Showers were taken, but as if by arrangement, no one retired for the night. The sitting room was full when Felicity emerged in her fuzzy socks and sweater to see where Carl had gone. Tich and her babies were doted upon, the food was sampled and drinks poured in a silence that felt more comfortable than words could express. The wheezing and whimpers of dreaming puppies and the crackle of the fire were the only sounds.

Felicity sat on Carl's lap in an overstuffed chair and surveyed the group over the brim of her cocoa mug. Naomi was nestled between Parker and Justin on the couch. Serena had been exiled to the floor at Justin's feet for fidgeting. Despite the position, there was nothing submissive in the way she watched him, and he blushed when he caught Felicity watching the both of them.

This is family, Felicity thought, and tears came up again. After twenty years, she was sitting at a proper hearth for Solstice again. Carl's hand slipped around her waist, and she leaned back into the comfort of his body.

His lips touched her neck. "Friends are the family we choose," he whispered. "Thank you for choosing this. For bringing all of us into your life."

Felicity wiped her eyes dry. *My own aggravating, annoying* precious *mind-reader*. "The clan increases," she whispered back. "We are blessed."

"Let's do this again," Serena said. "Soon."

Naomi said, "Without the fighting."

Serena made a face at her. "Spoilsport."

Naomi sighed, and Parker made a rude gesture at Serena.

Family. The weight of a contentment as warm and enveloping as any quilt settled over Felicity. "Spring Revel is in three months," she said. "We'll need to buy a tent or two."

The End

Carl Jenson: Master of emotional manipulation. His smile is one of his most dangerous weapons. He is his own worst enemy.

Felicity Chen: Crafter and entrepreneur. Knows her own mind, wears her heart on her sleeve.

Justin Wyatt:

Genius inventor, accidental executive, successful angel investor. Slowly losing a personal war against progressive brain damage.

Naomi Kwan

Looks breakable and timid. Isn't. Curious as a cat, slow to trust, loyal to a fault.

Parker (Eddie) Jenson

Security consultant and expert in the art of eliminating trouble. Long fuse with a homicidal temper at the end.

Serena Nguyen

Chaos is a personal specialty. Don't call her crazy.

Supporting Characters:

Some appear in person, others are only mentioned in passing

In Oregon

Assorted Chens, including Charity, Clement, Hope, Joy, Valiant, Victor, Will. (Don't worry about remembering everyone. Not even Felicity can keep track of them all.)

Bee, Cee, Dee, and Tee Geary

The Geary family takes charge of keeping the clan safe when they're on vacation.

Cousin Henry

Also known as Colonel. The useful connection. Every family has one.

Papa Joe

Clan patriarch. Unrepentant romantic, incorrigible schemer.

Uncle Dan

Not really an uncle. Dispenser of life advice.

In Nebraska & elsewhere

Alison (Allie) Gregorio

Office manager, people wrangler, and general all-around organizer. Gets it done.

Helen Armstrong

Brilliant actress. Once married to Justin Wyatt. Devoted to the goal of becoming richer and more famous than her rich, famous ex-husband.

Kaylie, Keene, and Terry

They work hard keep Justin and his secrets safe. Their security firm is named Mayhem & Havoc Incorporated. That says it all.

Ryan Armstrong Wyatt

Justin's son. Born in scandal, raised in fame's shadow. Too smart for his own good.

Tyler Burke

Genius, layabout, reader of graphic novels, Justin's work partner and self-proclaimed comic relief.

ABOUT THE AUTHOR

K. M. Herkes writes and publishes books that dance in the open spaces between science fiction and fantasy, specializing in stories about damaged souls, complicated lives, and triumphs of the spirit.

Professional development started with a Bachelor of Science degree in Biology and now includes experience in classroom teaching, animal training, aquaculture, horticulture, bookselling, and retail operations. Personal development is ongoing. Cats are involved.

When she isn't writing, she works at the Mount Prospect Public Library, digs holes in her backyard for fun, and enjoys experimental baking.

The author is online as @kemherkes@wandering.shop in the Fediverse, but mainly posts updates on her own website or via Patreon at patreon.com/kmherkes Visit dawnrigger.com for more information.

Join the mailing list at tinyletter.com/kmherkes for big book news and special alerts. Emails are never shared, sold, or spammed, and newsletters are roughly seasonal.